Chance Encounter

Kate Allenton

DEDICATION

To all of my readers who have been on the
Bennett journey with me from the beginning.

Thank you!

Chance Encounter

ACKNOWLEDGMENTS

This book would not be in existence without the love and support of my family and friends who gave me the gentle nudge needed to see this through. I appreciate each and every one of you.

CHAPTER 1

John Bennett rubbed his tired eyes as he moved through his Aunt Claire's foyer. Royal blue and yellow streamers swirled, dipping from the ceiling toward the floor. Shiny silver, helium-filled balloons lined the marble entryway in celebratory fashion. The official colors of the FBI logo were bold and in his face. He would know. The job had been his dream since childhood. He pushed the thoughts away, taking in the rest of the décor. She'd out done herself again. She was "that" aunt. It was her style, and she would tell you it was her pleasure. Aunts, uncles, and cousins of all ages milled past the foyer, most oblivious to him watching from a safe distance. Sleep was calling him. Sleep he'd been lacking and severely missed ever since dreaming about the mysterious woman who plagued his nights.

"She" was an unknown. "She" was in trouble. "She" was going to be a pain in his ass. Two weeks of visions and he'd yet to figure out where or who the hell "she" was so he could save her life and finally release whatever mysterious hold she held over his sanity. Maybe the next vision would come complete with road signs or a treasure map. A GPS function would work too, anything that would get him closer to figuring out what the heck was going on and give him a plan of action to fix her problem. He could thank his mom for the frustration that she referred to as a gift. The super mojo blood that held these specific traits had been passed down through her bloodlines. His dad was just as normal as normal could be for an FBI agent, nothing like the loons down his mother's branch of the ancestry tree.

Special gifts were reserved for superheroes, not the everyday people that he called family. His gift...the visions in his dreams had served their purpose when they'd been about his family, and only his family, but now unknowns were in play. He gritted his teeth and shook his head. To hell with that, to hell with "her". Find her, fix her, and move on. That was why he was here, well that and to confess his secrets to his parents.

"Congratulations." His uncle, Butch Edwards, said while grasping his shoulder and steering him farther into the line of fire, otherwise known as the elaborate party being thrown in John's honor. "There's no turning back now." He leaned in to whisper, "Just indulge them. If it makes your Aunt Claire happy, it makes me happy."

"Uncle Butch, we both know she went to too much trouble." They stepped out into the expansive, open living room where everyone else was relaxing. The place looked like a museum. Breakables everywhere, fine china, and crystal. Aunt Claire was just begging for trouble since all of Johns' cousins were running amuck.

"You should see what she has planned for the Christmas party," Butch mumbled before patting John's back. "Being the oldest sister, she's the self-appointed matriarch and official party planner. She'll tell you it's her God-given right to dote on her nieces and nephews. It's part of life, buddy. So just suck it up and smile."

"You won't hear me complain. She helped me track down Mom's present."

Butch grinned. "I know. We both had to call in a lot of favors for that little doozy."

"My baby!" John's mom called from across the room. Her hands flew into the air and she made a beeline right for him, giving him only seconds until impact. She flung her arms around him, squeezing him tight in a bone-crushing hug. He didn't need oxygen to survive...just the love of a mother...right?

He hugged her back, but she didn't let go.   One day she would, but apparently today wasn't that day.

"Mom..." He patted her back. "You can let go now."

His mom harrumphed.

"Abby...you're going to squeeze the life out of our son. Let him go, already," John's dad, Sam, chided her. "He's not a kid anymore, honey. He's a grown man."

His mom's lips pursed, sending an unspoken challenge to her husband. Sam grinned and held up his hands, stepping back. "Sorry, son, you have to learn to pick your battles, and this isn't one I'm ready to die for."

This was what John had come back for. This was what was missing in his life - the unconditional love from his family. Well this...and finding "her."

Abby loosened her hold but kept her arm around his waist, leaning into his side. The top of her brunette head barely reached John's shoulders. She'd always been overprotective of him. He'd lucked out in the parents department and no one would ever normally hear him complain. Today might very well be different.

Tossing his arm around his mom's shoulder, John grinned. "Lighten up, Dad. I'll always be her baby."

"That title was stolen from you ten years ago," John's little brother, Dixon, said with a smirk in passing. "That belongs to me, now."

The little shit.

"Dream on, punk. I'll always be her first and favorite son," John called after him.

"Knock it off, you two. You're both my babies." His mom released his waist and threaded her arm around his. "Let's go get you a drink and you can tell me all about how well your interview went."

This was the moment he'd dreaded the entire drive over. Disappointing her wasn't something he ever liked to do.

She steered him into the enormous kitchen. Lots of windows surrounded the room, letting in the natural light of the day, all the better to watch his expressions. She'd see every grimace on his face and so would his aunts who were seated at the table sipping coffee. Just perfect. Odds were against him. Three against one. He'd lose every time.

An island counter stood in the middle of the room, separating the kitchen counters and the breakfast table. Maybe he'd take up residence on the other side so, when he broke his news, his mother wasn't within arm's length. Copper pots and pans were strung precariously overhead. Potted plants lined the tops of the cabinets. The recessed lighting of the cabinets gave the room a very open, relaxing feel. Maybe the ambiance would help his cause. Who was he kidding?

Abby gestured toward the table where Emma and Claire were seated, watching him. Did they already know? Sweat beaded on his brow, but he didn't make a move to wipe it. "Have a seat. What do you want to drink?"

"You don't have to wait on me, Mom. I can get it myself." John answered even as he sat down.

"Don't be ridiculous." She stood drumming her fingers against the fridge door, waiting.

"How about a beer?" He could use the liquid courage as his crutch to confess his sins.

"How about I'll make you some coffee, instead? Judging by the bags beneath your eyes, it looks like you can use it." Abby moved to the coffee pot and started pouring two mugs. "Didn't they ever let you sleep?"

If she only knew.

Claire leaned over and hugged him. "Congratulations, sweet pea."

"Congratulations, squirt," Emma echoed while winking. "We all knew it was just a matter of time before the FBI realized it's in your blood."

It was in his blood all right, with his mom being a forensic investigator and his dad working as an agent for the same division of the FBI that John had initially applied for and had worked his ass off to get in. Their unfounded praise left John swallowing around his uncomfortably dry throat. Hell, forget the beer, he needed a shot. Unease settled in his gut. They weren't just going to be disappointed when they learned the truth; they'd start doing what his mom and aunts did best. They'd start making plans to fix his problems.

Aunt Emma leaned back in her chair. "What?" She turned to look into the empty space behind her. "You've got to be kidding me!"

She continued to talk to who John could only assume was Momma Mae, the infamous ghost that only Aunt Emma and Uncle Jake could see. A ghost that liked to talk in riddles...and a damn ghost that was probably tattle-telling on him right this minute. Crap.

Aunt Emma spun around, nailing him with a look that told him he'd guessed right. The cat was out of the bag. His secret was blown, and he had a damn ghost to thank for ratting him out.

"Jonathan Maxwell Bennett!" his father's voice bellowed from the adjoining room, and then he walked into the kitchen with the phone pressed up against his ear.

"Yes, sir...Yes, sir. I'll see what I can do. I understand he performed at the top of his recruiting class and you were looking forward to having him on your team." He leveled John with his fatherly—you've-screwed-up-and-you-*will-*   fix-this—glare. "Yes, sir, I'll give him the message. Thank you for calling."

John slowly rose from his seat, holding up his hands in surrender. It might help, and it couldn't hurt to try, while reasoning with the natives he called mom and dad. "I can explain."

Confused, his mom glanced back and forth between them both.

The decision had been the right one. He was sure of it at the time but, after seeing the disappointed look first-hand on his father's face, he wasn't quite so sure now.

Abby set her mug down. "What?" She moved to John's side, where she'd been his entire life, his silent cheerleader in her own way. She just preferred guns to pompoms and dead guys to football players. It was in her blood too; maybe he had screwed up.

"Tell me," she said, breaking the awkward silence.

His dad's brows hitched a fraction. John knew that look: the barely contained, ready to skin you alive and string you up because you just royally screwed up look. "Well...what are you waiting for? I'll let you tell her. You're a grown man, obviously capable of making your own decisions. Time to man up, kid."

Emma silently rose from where she'd been sitting and took Claire by the arm. She hitched her thumb over her shoulder. "We're just going to give you some privacy."

Claire dug in her heels, stopping Emma from the retreat. "No, we're not. I want to hear this."

Emma nodded toward the door. "I'll fill you in."

Perfect. His aunts wouldn't be the barricade he'd been counting on. He was now officially fair game and his mom was going to kill him. He let out a long sigh and turned to face his mother, the only person whose opinion he valued just as much as his own. "The FBI offered me a job, and I turned them down."

Abby's brows dipped, as she was unable to hide the confusion from showing on her face. "Why?" She glanced over John's shoulder in Sam's direction, possibly looking for answers his dad wouldn't have. Only seconds ticked by before her gaze resettled on John's face. "I thought this was what you wanted. You've worked your whole life for this opportunity. What happened? Why aren't you taking the offer?"

John gestured to a chair and waited for his mom to sit. "It's complicated."

Abby folded her arms and leaned forward. "If there is one thing we Bennetts understand, it's that life is complicated. So just spill it."

"There's this girl..."

"Oh, for the love of God." Abby flew from her chair. The quick movement sent the chair careening out from beneath her, almost knocking it to the ground. Her hands flew up in the air as she cut off his explanation. "You haven't gotten one pregnant, have you? Please don't tell me some bimbo talked you out of your dream. If she's pregnant, we will help both of you."

"Mother!" John broke in as soon as his mom took a breath. He ran a hand through his short hair and tried for a calmer, more logical approach. "No, Mom, no one is pregnant. You aren't having grandchildren, and no one has talked me into giving this up."

His mom released a long sigh. "I'm not judging you, baby. I'm just trying to understand." Her gaze bore a hole into his, as if searching his soul for the answers she needed. "Who is she?"

His dad moved to the fridge, grabbed two beers, popped the tops, and handed one to John.

"I don't know who she is."

Abby righted the chair and sat down, pinching the bridge of her nose before picking up her coffee. It was clear she was trying to keep her composure. It was a miracle in the making. She sipped. "Okay...we're listening."

Finally, those were the words he'd been waiting for. Not that he had any idea of how they were going to react. Better than the last five minutes, he hoped.

He took a long draw of his beer while he tried to make sense in his own mind before attempting to explain stuff he didn't even understand himself. "I keep dreaming of her. She's running from someone or something, and I think she needs my help."

His dad sat down next to his mom and laid his arm over the back of her chair. His fingers settled on her shoulder. John noticed the silent support and gave a slight nod in his father's direction. Abby had missed out on eighteen years of his dad's support after John was born. It wasn't his dad's fault. He had been trying to protect her from a serial killer.

"And why can't you help her if you're working for the FBI? You might actually be able to give her more assistance, have better resources."

Valid, logical questions. He was getting somewhere now. "The places in my dreams are here in Southall. I can't ignore these dreams, Mom. You've taught me better than that. Besides, I've got this feeling she's important. The FBI wants to station me in Washington. I can't leave...not yet."

Abby took the beer from Sam's hand and took a sip before passing it back. "John...you know we love you, and we'll do everything we can to help this girl when you find her, but why is she special? The only other dreams you've ever had were of our family. What do you think changed?"

John shrugged. "I don't know."

He lied while rubbing at the small scar on the side of his stomach. The healed indentation was his constant reminder why finding her was important. If he'd come clean about why things had changed, then he'd have to come clean about a whole lot more. And he had no desire to die today. His mother, Abby Bennett, was going to skin him alive when she figured it out.

Emma's ten-year-old daughter, Lily, bounced into the kitchen and over to the fridge. She pushed her unruly blonde curls out of her baby blue eyes. As a baby, she'd looked like a doll, a cherub that prompted old ladies everywhere to ooh and ahh. Now that she was a bit older, her attitude had started to shine through. Lily was definitely her mother's daughter. She was a Bennett through and through. Bullies hated her; small children loved her; and she'd defend anyone who needed her help. John couldn't be more proud of the kid she was turning out to be. She was an old soul in a little body. At an early age, Lily, like her mother, could talk to dead people; and yet, she'd embraced it just the same.

Lily grabbed a soda, popped the top, and stepped over to the table. "Delaney's mom wants me to warn you to watch out for her right hook. If she hits you, you'll never ever see her again."

John exchanged a look with his mom. "Lily, who is Delaney and where did you meet her mom?"

Lily pointed over John's shoulder. "She's right behind you. She's the dead woman wearing the red ball gown just like Aunt Claire's."

Lily glanced past John's shoulder to the far corner of the kitchen. Her brows dipped. "She's only been dead for a year...She keeps fading in and out." Lily shrugged her shoulders.

"She's gone now, but she's been bugging me all week. Maybe now she'll go away since I passed you her message." Lily grinned and started walking backward out of the kitchen. "The rose. She kept repeating...the rose, and no...before you even ask...I have no idea what the crazy, dressed-up dead lady is talking about." Lily shook her head. "She's worse than Momma Mae when it comes to giving answers. It must be a ghost thing." Lily shrugged as if contemplating her assumption.

Once again left alone with his parents, John was even more confused, but at least he had a name for the woman. "Delaney," he whispered, letting her name roll from his tongue, getting a taste for it and filing it in his brain.

Abby rose from her chair. "How old does she look in your dream?"

"My age, give or take two years in either direction."

Abby nodded. "Well, that's something." Abby dumped the coffee in the sink. "Seems like I've got some work to do if we're going to find your girl. I'll need some specifics. Hair color, eye color, any visible identifying marks you can make out from the vision. A sketch artist will help give us a face to put with the name."

And in seconds flat, his mother had turned from overly dramatic about his decision, to mother of the year and in full work mode. John's heart clenched with appreciation. He loved her more than anything. "Mom...you don't have to do this."

Abby pressed a kiss to the top of his head. "Yes, I do, honey. You're my baby. I'll always help you. It's my right as your mom, so   no   arguing."

CHAPTER 2

Two long grueling weeks and John was no closer to meeting his mystery woman, yet he had a new job to add to his resume. Working for his Uncle Jake, at Tactical Maneuvers, was the right decision for now. He'd spent countless hours trying to help his mom figure out who exactly Delaney might be. Wasted, countless hours that hadn't turned up any fresh clues. Today promised to be different; today everything was going to change.

He'd scoured the streets of his hometown looking for the dilapidated building in his dream. He checked his watch one last time. The time was right; the place was right; and when a raindrop splashed on his windshield, it confirmed that the day was right.

He glanced up the street and spotted her instantly. Her long blonde hair was pulled back into a ponytail, a deviation from the dream, but he wouldn't let that minor detail make him deviate from his determination. She glanced over her shoulder, while biting her bottom lip, before quickening her pace.

John's gaze travelled up and down the street as he tried to figure the source of her unrest. No one was chasing her. She had little to worry about with him watching her back, even if she didn't know it.

Pulling his Glock out of his holster, he checked the clip before shoving it back inside, where it would be concealed by his jacket. He didn't want to scare her. He was here to help. John tapped the steering wheel while he waited for her to enter the alleyway.

"Here goes nothing." He stepped out of the SUV and headed across the street, stopping to peer around the corner. Voices drifted on the late evening wind as thunder rolled above. A storm was coming. He had to make this quick. A chill skirted down his spine from the late December air.

"Where's my stuff?" Delaney demanded.

"Shit, you aren't supposed to be here," the guy in the alley growled. His head swiveled around as he looked up and down the alley.

"Did you think you could hide from me forever, Vinnie?" he heard her ask.

"This isn't a good time, Del."

The woman from his dreams shoved Vinnie up against the wall. "It wasn't a good time when you screwed me with your last information. My boss was pissed."

Her arm went to Vinnie's throat and she leaned forward, pressing on the guy's windpipe.

"I can't talk about this now, Del," the guy squeaked out as he gasped for air.

The man was big enough that he could have pushed her away, yet he stayed at her mercy. What the hell was going on?

John's dream was playing out before his eyes. He knew what would happen next, and it was time to step in if he had any chance at saving her life.

Rubbing his neck, he took a deep breath and stepped out into the alleyway. "Excuse me."

Both sets of eyes turned on him. Delaney pinned him with a glare while Vinnie's eyes bulged, his face turning red.

"Who the hell are you!" she demanded as John held up his hands and continued to walk toward her.

"I'm here to help you," John answered. He gestured toward the guy. "You might want to let him breathe."

Delaney glanced to Vinnie and narrowed her eyes, even as she eased her grip. "Do you know this guy?"

He shook his head.

Delaney dropped her hold on the guy and turned toward John. "Listen, I don't know who you are, but this is none of your business."

Vinnie sputtered for air, coughing as he grabbed his throat. He rested his hands on his knees before righting and shoving her into the brick wall. Dirt and crumbled debris drifted down on her head. Vinnie took off down the alleyway, disappearing out onto the road.

"Great." She righted herself, brushing off the fallen grime and debris. "He got away, thanks to you."

"Thanks to me, you're both going to live." John grabbed her hand in a tight grip and started leading her out of the alley.

"What are you..." Her words trailed off when she glanced behind her.

"Saving your ass." John looked over his shoulder, confirming what he already knew. Three big burly guys in black leather jackets stood at the other end of the alley. "I'd ask if they were your friends, but I know they aren't."

Delaney quit resisting and hurried to keep in step. John finally released his hold when he reached the SUV. "Those guys are going to kill you if you don't come with me."

She hesitated while John was getting in the driver's side.

"You have about two seconds to decide."

She glanced back once more, her gaze never leaving the alleyway as she rounded the SUV and climbed into the passenger seat.

"Buckle up, this may get bumpy."

John started the ignition and gunned the gas as a black sedan pulled up at the entrance of the alleyway. He watched in the rearview mirror as the guys from the alley climbed in. Delaney was turned around in her seat, watching through the back window.

"Hold on," John demanded as he squealed around the street corner.

Delaney turned around and grabbed the oh-shit handle as John sped up and down alleyways in an effort to ditch the guys that were after her.

"Who are you?" she asked her voice shaky.

"I'm John, but you can call me the cavalry." He chanced a glance at her. "And it looks like I arrived just in the nick of time."

John knew the roads like the backs of his hands and with good reason. He'd grown up on these streets. He shoved the gas pedal down harder and turned down three more streets before pulling into a parking garage. He backed the SUV into a spot and killed the lights. He'd seen this play out in several different scenarios, and this parking garage was the only one where they wouldn't get caught.

"Listen, I don't know who you are, or how you knew that was going to happen, but I don't need your help." Delaney flicked off her seatbelt, threw open the passenger door, and hurried out the other side. John followed her out and rounded the vehicle, not giving her a moment to disappear.

She was quick, but he'd been expecting it. He grabbed her arm while watching her figure out her escape. "I'm one of the good guys. Let me help you."

She snatched her arm out of his grip and backed away from him. "You've helped enough."

Pulling a gun out of her purse, she pointed it at him. "Not another step, asshole." She stepped around him and walked backward toward the garage entrance.

John was left with no other choice but to watch her leave and hope that the little help he'd given her was enough to give him back his dreams. He'd find out soon enough.

He got back into the SUV and pulled out of the garage as lightning lit the darkening sky. The rain fell hard and fast; John wondered if Delaney was getting soaked. He drove slowly down the street, trying to locate her to make sure she was all right, but she'd disappeared just as quickly as he'd found her. John headed home to his bed.

His phone rang and, when he answered, his mother's tone was full of concern. "I take it you found her."

"Yeah, how did you know?"

"Aunt Emma started the phone chain when her cramps started."

"I found her and saved her from the guys in my dream."

"Is she with you?"

Was she with him? What a joke. In all of the times he'd dreamed about her, he never saw the outcome, only them ditching the guys with the guns. If he had, he might have been prepared. "No, as soon as we lost the guys chasing her, she pulled a gun on me."

"What! Are you okay?"

"I'm fine, Mom. I tried to stop her. I can't say I blame her. Some random guy on the street knows about an attempt on her life? I wouldn't have trusted me either."

"Well, hopefully, that's the end of her danger and you can finally get on with your life."

His mind reeled with confusion and the ramifications of his actions. Was she truly gone? Would he ever find out the answers and why she'd even appeared? "I'll call you if she invades my dreams tonight. But maybe that's the last of her."

"Be careful, John. I love you."

"I will. I love you too."

John arrived home and made a mad dash to his door through the pouring rain. He shook the water from his head before he walked inside and ditched his coat and keys in the entryway. A hot shower was calling his name. He needed something to remove the chill and warm his soul. He took his shower and emerged ten minutes later, nice and fresh. He changed into track pants, ate a bowl of soup, and plopped down in front of the television to watch football for the night. He fought his tired eyes in an attempt to finish watching the remainder of the game, but to no avail. They slid shut, and it wasn't long before he was dreaming again, dreaming of her.

Sun shining through the open curtains warmed his face, pulling him out of the dream he'd been having. He rolled onto his back, wiping the sleep from his eyes and stared up at the ceiling. A long, exasperated breath left his lips. "I guess today is round two."

He rolled off the couch, showered, and got ready for the day. He fixed a cup of coffee and sipped. The dark brew warmed his throat and helped ease his muscles from the restless night of sleep. He'd dreamed of her again, and he knew where she'd show up today. He'd paid more attention this time and picked up on the clues. In his dream, he was signing the credit card receipt for the dagger he'd been going to purchase; he'd double-checked the place from the receipt, the time stamp, and even the purchase price. He'd never imagined the next meeting would be over a weapon, the same weapon from his dream in months prior. His mother's Christmas present to be exact. After dressing, he glanced down at his watch. He had twenty minutes before he needed to be where he knew he'd find her. Twenty more minutes and he'd be one step closer to getting this woman out of his mind. She was in trouble, regardless of whether she knew it or not. He'd help her, just so he could get back to his own life. Whatever was left of it. John slid the black trench coat on, straightened his tie, and grabbed his keys. He had a destiny to meet, and he wouldn't be late.

****

"You can't do that." An accusatory voice came from the door as John handed Mac, the pawn shop owner, his credit card as payment for his purchase.

John turned around, noting Mac and he were no longer the only people in the store. He wasn't shocked; it was her. He'd been expecting her.

"You again!" Delaney narrowed her eyes. "Are you following me?"

He shrugged. "Hard to do, considering I got here first. So do you care to clue me in on what I can't do?"

She stomped over to the counter. He'd seen how this played out. His vision had warned him, and he'd known she'd show up. Let the games begin.

She glanced down at the jewel-encrusted ceremonial knife John had been plagued, as if by fate, to buy for his mom as her Christmas present. "You can't buy that."

John crossed his arms over his chest. "Oh...is that so?"

She nodded. "It's mine."

John had dreamt weeks earlier about his mother's gift, yet it wasn't until last night that Delaney had surfaced in that particular dream. In all of the pawnshops in the entire world, it was serendipitous the knife he wanted ended up in the store not a mile from his house. His mother didn't normally like antiques, but she'd be thrilled with this one, and John didn't care how beautiful the little spitfire was that wanted to argue ownership. No...the blonde was wrong. It wasn't hers; it was his.

Mac laid the receipt in front of John for his signature. Without glancing up, John asked as he signed, "Hey, Mac, is this lady the one who pawned the knife?"

John knew the answer to that question before he even asked. He'd tried to track the knife down from the simple dream. He'd drawn it; he'd researched it; yet it wasn't until recently that he'd figured out where to find it. In his research, he'd found tales of this piece. The ceremonial dagger had been stolen two decades ago and the mystery had gone unsolved, along with the dagger's location. A few concurrent nights of sleep and John had put most of the pieces together. He knew exactly where to find it. The dagger was within his reach and in his town. The piece resurfaced with some minor changes to camouflage the real identity. The dagger was real, along with the theft, and it was in his grasp. By Christmas morning, with the use of her abilities, his mom would know exactly what had happened to the piece all those years ago. Solving an age-old crime would appease her curiosity since she'd never be able to reveal where the information came from.

Mac propped his elbows on the counter, and his gaze slid up and down Delaney's body in a cursory fashion. "Nope, I bought it from the auction of an estate sale. I've never seen this woman before in my life."

John picked up the duplicate receipt and waved it in the air as he grinned. "Sorry, Del...looks like you're wrong. This is now mine."

Delaney's eyes filled with tears. Her lips slightly trembled. A tear slipped free, running down her cheek. He'd underestimated her. She was good. The move was award worthy, priceless and almost believable. Almost.

"I don't know how you know me, but it's mine. That dagger is a family heirloom. It was my mother's." A second tear slid down the same path. "I'll double whatever you paid for it."

John's lips twitched, but he held back his smile. This woman was a gifted actress all right. Turning the waterworks on and off, like a spigot in the sink, took talent. She narrowed her eyes and folded her arms against her chest, closing herself off from his scrutiny. She was lying. He'd trained to spot the telltale signs. The question was why she wanted the dagger. He slid the box into the inside pocket of his coat. He watched her eyes tracking the movement. Her jaw ticked, and her eyes momentarily narrowed before she slid her mask firmly back into place, returning her expression to that of a hurt woman. "How about we go get a cup of coffee, and you can tell me the story of how it ended up in the pawn shop."

"I don't think so. I don't even know your name and I don't drink with strangers."

"My name's John Bennett and I'm not a stranger. I'm the owner of the dagger."

She lowered her head and clasped her fingers in front of her. "One cup of coffee?" She looked up at him through wet lashes.

"And then you'll let me buy the knife from you?"

This lady was a piece of work. Her imaginary sob story was going to be good. Granted, full of crap...but nonetheless entertaining. And today, he was ready to be entertained.

"I'll consider it, but I'm not making any promises. This is for a special woman." Two could play her game.

John held open the door and followed behind her out of the shop.

"You know, you're not as intimidating without a gun in your hand."

"Gee, thanks. Are you going to tell me how you knew to find me in the alley?"

"Nope. Just be glad I did."

While passing a man dressed up as Santa and ringing a bell, John pulled some dollar bills from his pocket. He stuffed them into the slit at the top of the little red hanging bucket.

"Bless you child; Merry Christmas."

"Merry Christmas," John replied.

She glanced over at him while he was pulling the door open to the Starlight Café, his Aunt Emma's coffee shop. Light music played in the background as the aromas of cinnamon and freshly brewed coffee drifted to his nose. Gold and green flickering lights were strung around the café, and the workers were wearing red and white felt Santa hats. Both men and women, with shopping bags on the floor at their feet, occupied the tables. The air was alive and hopeful with the Christmas spirit.

They placed their orders at the counter, paid, and took their coffees to a table farthest away from the crowd and the prying ears of Mrs. A., a family friend and the town gossip. John had picked the table situated near the windows for reasons she wouldn't see coming. He knew the security camera would get a good look at her face. He'd be able to get a full ID on her with the facial recognition software he had at his disposal. He was going to enjoy watching her performance. "Smile."

"Excuse me."

John pointed up to the camera strategically pointed at the table he'd chosen. "You're on candid camera." He leaned forward. "The gig is up, Delaney. Why don't you start with explaining why you're lying about the knife and who you're running from?"

Her mouth parted before she snapped it closed. "Not until you tell me how you know my name."

"You wouldn't believe me if I told you." John leaned back and sipped his coffee. He watched her, cataloging every minuscule movement she made. Her gaze darted around the room as she brushed her hair behind her ears. Her fingers nervously tore at the napkin in front of her. She was acting like a caged animal on the verge of extinction. "You first; why the lie?"

Delaney smirked and, abandoning the mutilated napkin, she crossed her arms over her chest. "You may know my name, but that's all. There's no way you know my reason." Her brow lifted, and her lips twitched as she picked up her coffee, sipping the hot brew.

She was right. He knew very little about her, but all of that was about to change. "You're right. I know little else but your name and the fact you needed saving." He cocked his head to the side. "If you don't count the fact that I know you want the knife." Her smile slipped. "And I own it."

Her smug expression had now turned into a fully formed frown. She sat quietly, her eyes on everyone and everything in the room, except him. She released a long sigh and leaned back, crossing her legs. "Okay...you got me. My name is Delaney Chance."

"And the knife, Ms. Chance?" John asked, wanting to put all of the pieces of her involvement together.

She glanced around before leaning forward in her seat. Her brows dipped as she answered in hushed tones. "You're not going to believe me."

John knew crazy, and she wasn't it. There wasn't anything she could say that would surprise him.

"I'm a reporter, and I have reason to believe that knife may have been used to commit a crime," she whispered.

"Excuse me?"

She let out an exasperated breath. "I said it was a weapon used in a crime."

Now he was getting somewhere. He'd researched it. He knew the dagger's history and had researched the origins. Hell, even the pawn dealer knew its value and John had paid through the nose to get the piece. What he didn't know was where it had gone when it was stolen from the collector and where it had been hiding all of this time. That was the sole purpose of giving the piece to his mom. One touch and she'd know the truth, transported back to that moment in time, via her mind, to witness a potential piece of history. Buying it was a calculated risk but, if the ability it represented was real, then the purchase was priceless.

"And what's your proof, Ms. Chance?"

She shrugged and bit her bottom lip. He was trained to watch for body language. He had actually been top of his class in being able to pick out a liar. She met his gaze. "You chased off the guy that was going to give me the proof, of the crime, that I needed. Listen, you have to trust that I'm trying to make things right."

"I don't know you. Why would I trust you?"

"I'm not a bad person, Mr. Bennett, just in a shitty predicament, and I need the dagger to get myself out."

She meant what she'd said. She believed what she'd said. That still didn't answer what she was running from or why she'd taken up residence in his dreams every single time he closed his eyes.

"What are you running from, Delaney Chance?"

The bell above the door chimed. The newcomer drew her gaze and held it, prompting John to glance over his shoulder. A short, muscular guy dressed in jeans and a black leather jacket stood next to a tall woman with molasses colored hair. The pair looked eerily familiar although John couldn't put his finger on who they were. The man shifted and silver glinted from the gun stashed out of sight. He looked like one of the guys from last night. Hit men? Police? Drug dealers? Endless possibilities ran through John's mind. Wait. John paused; his gaze flew back to the man's face. Recognition punched him like a fist to the gut and, if John was right, Delaney Chance was in way over her head. The couple turned slowly as they scanned the area and patrons.

John turned back around to find the other side of the booth empty. "Son of a bitch."

There was only one other exit out of the café, and he'd be damned if he let her get away. He slid from the booth in time to find Delaney panicked in the hallway. A six-foot blonde, Amazon-looking lady had Delaney pinned against the wall, her hands trapping Delaney on both sides of her head.

John strode down the hall with new purpose. "You make new friends everywhere we go, don't you, baby?"

He held out his hand to Delaney and she took it, sliding beneath the blonde's arm. From a distance, he'd thought the blonde was pretty, not his type, but pretty in an Amazon kind of way. The closer he'd gotten to her, the more he had realized how wrong he'd been. The creases in her face were deep, and the bags beneath her eyes made them look hollow. She could use another dye job on her roots to cover the black streaks, and she smelled like an ashtray.

"Are you going to introduce me to your new friend, honey?"

Delaney moved to his side. "She's not a friend." She glanced up at him. Anger filled her eyes. Her lips pulled into a fine line. "We're going to be late for our appointment, babe."

John threw his arm over her shoulder and kissed the top of her head. "We can't have that now, can we?"

He tipped his head at the Amazon. Delaney's body was stiff beneath his touch, and he silently wondered if it was from the contact or from those people that had come in looking for her. He rounded the corner out of sight, heading for the back exit, and glanced over his shoulder. The hall was empty. They weren't being followed. Not yet. He pulled her into Aunt Emma's office and closed the door, locking it behind him.

"What are you doing?"

"Saving your ass...again." He gestured to one of the leather seats as he pulled the phone out of his pocket and started punching numbers. He moved around Aunt Emma's desk and hit the keys on the computer, pulling up a still of the three intruders talking out in the café. A grin split his lips.

"Uncle Jake. I'm sending you an image of three people in Aunt Emma's café. I think they're the ones after Delaney. Can you run them for me and call me back with the details? Make sure you check them against dad's database. I'm holed up in Aunt Emma's office with Delaney, and we need an extraction."

"Aunt Emma? What the hell is going on here?" Delaney demanded as she stood and stepped closer to the wall monitor with the still of the blonde, the brunette, and the biker.

"Perfect timing. Tell him I'll be ready. I'll be bringing her out the back exit in two minutes." He slid his finger against the screen to end the call, made a few more clicks on the keyboard, and stepped around the desk. He glanced down at his watch as the seconds ticked by. Seconds that seemed to feel like forever. He grabbed her hand. "On my mark...five, four, three, two..."

He never got to one because the fire alarm blared throughout the café and nearby buildings. John peeked out of the office door. The blinking red lights flashed, lighting up the darkened hallway. Jake had warned that he was taking the power out in a one-block radius while he sent in a plain-clothed team to follow those three people. The confusion would give John and Delaney time to sneak out the back entrance to meet Butch at the extraction point. It had been pure luck that the team was even nearby. Either luck or one of his relatives' gifts had played a part. His money was on his Aunt Emma's interference.

He led her down the hall in front of him, blocking her body from any prying eyes that remained in the building. He pushed through the exit door and became momentarily blinded by the afternoon sun before he helped her into the waiting SUV owned by Tactical Maneuvers that was driven personally by Butch.

John pulled the door closed behind him and met Butch's gaze.

John nodded once. "It's time we get moving." Butch threw the SUV into gear and pulled out onto a street that ran parallel to Main Street. It would take them farther away from the center of town. Farther away from the thugs that had scared her.

"You know Jake's going to catch hell for that little stunt, right?"

John settled into the leather seat and watched the confusion play across Delaney's face.

"I'll offer my babysitting services. That should appease both Aunt Emma and Jake."

Butch chuckled. "Well played, kid."

Delaney turned in her seat, glancing out the back window before swiveling back around. "You can just drop me off at the next corner and I'll walk back to my hotel."

She wasn't from Southall. He should have seen that one coming. He suspected the other three, that appeared to have business with her, weren't from Southall either. "We're taking you to a secure location until we get all of this sorted out."

"They have a name for what you're doing...it's called kidnapping." She took a deep breath and clutched at the locket on her necklace. "Listen, I appreciate what you did back there, but I'll be fine." She unzipped her purse and pulled out a wad of cash and held it out. "If you'll just hand over the knife, I'll be out of your hair before the sun goes down." She gave a fake smile that didn't reach her eyes. "Doesn't that sound nice....hmm?"

John grinned. "I'm not taking your money and we're not holding you against your will, Ms. Chance. You're free to leave whenever you want...but let me make one thing perfectly clear. You'll be leaving without *my* property."

She snapped her parted mouth closed and shoved the cash back into her purse, zipping it shut. "Why...of all the nerve..."

"Honey...you have no clue." John turned toward the window and watched the passing scenery as they got closer and closer to Tactical headquarters nestled securely on his Aunt Claire's property.

"Uncle Butch, please pull over at the corner," John requested.

The SUV came to a stop next to the curb. John held her gaze. "It's your call, princess. You can leave now and head back into town, or you can stay with us, where you'll be safe until we get this sorted out."

She momentarily hesitated while still clutching her pendant. Her eyes clenched shut. "Fine." When she opened them again, her eyes pierced him with her demand. "But I want a closer look at that knife. Do we have a deal?"

John nodded. "Yep...we've got a deal."

CHAPTER 3

Delaney was in deep trouble, and it just kept getting worse. Her boss thought she was crazy; she'd let the knife slip through her fingers; the Jessup clan had tracked her down much quicker than the last time, and now it appeared she was stuck with John Bennett and his covert operations family that liked to play spies. Just perfect.

Delaney tightened her hold on the purse strapped across her chest. The weight of the gun pressing against her chest reassured her that she was marginally safe. Her nerves were skyrocketing out of control. They'd offered her an out, but leaving John defeated the whole purpose of coming to this God-forsaken town in the first place.

One way or another, she was leaving with that damn knife.

The SUV rolled to a stop in front of a tall security fence. A well-muscled man stepped out of the security shack with his finger on the trigger of a machine gun. The guard gave Butch a nod and, a few seconds later, they were driving through the iron gate. What the hell had she gotten herself into? A stone wall surrounded the property. The only entrance and exit, as far as she could tell, was the one they'd driven through. What could be so important that it was hidden behind all this security? The idea of another story popped into her head. Outing the security compound and what lay inside might be a whole new story of a higher caliber. She held in her smile. Her boss might even approve of the story, if she still had her job when she returned.

The car stopped and she got out following behind John, who held her future in the palm of his hand—well, technically, in his coat pocket—she silently wondered how he'd known her name and where to find her. Hell, how he'd known she was in trouble and running. These were all answers she'd find out before she skipped town, with the guy's knife, after finding the other piece of the puzzle. He'd make interesting fodder in her story. If nothing else, his reasoning on why he'd purchased the stolen heirloom intrigued her. Hadn't he said it was for a woman? What kind of a woman wanted a weapon as a gift? She was doing John a favor by taking it off his hands. Whoever the woman was, she might just thank her. Hell, did he even realize what he had purchased?

John slowed to walk by Delaney's side. "These are more than my co-workers. They're my family, so please, play nice."

Had he just suggested that she wouldn't? "Where are you taking me?"

"To the inner sanctum." John chuckled. "You'll be required to submit a blood sample before we give you access to all of our secrets."

Was this guy on crack? Had he taken a dose of the crazy while she wasn't looking?

Delaney lightly touched John's arm, stopping him.

"Lighten up, Delaney; it was a joke. You're in the Tactical Maneuvers compound, just outside of town. And although it is state of the art, they won't require your blood sample, and I'm sure Uncle Jake won't be telling you all of our secrets. Just relax. I haven't let anything happen to you yet, and I'm not about to start now. You have my word."

"Yeah...and what's that worth?"

John pressed his lips together and crossed his arms. "Everything I am and everything I'll ever be. My word is the only thing that I have, and I'm giving it to you freely, Delaney. Don't take it for granted."

He turned and started back down the hall, no longer waiting around to see if she'd follow. She double stepped to catch up to him as they entered a huge room. Monitors surrounded the walls, some of various places in town and some looked to be satellite images tracking heat signatures. The place was impressive. She'd immediately thought FBI field office with all of the Intel they looked to be gathering. Maybe the knife wasn't the story at all. Maybe it *was* these guys.

"Who are these guys?" she mumbled.

A man in fatigues greeted them and steered them to a conference room. He pulled the door closed behind them, effectively closing them off, the secrets she wanted to uncover in the other room.

"FBI? No wait." She held up her hand. "CIA?" She nodded happily with her choice. "You're some super-secret division of the CIA that the general population doesn't know about."

John rolled his eyes but politely pulled out her chair. Chivalry? The surprises just kept coming.

She sat and gazed around the room, looking for any other exits. "So tell me," she said, turning back to John. "Do you guys fight the things that go bump in the night? Is that why I've never heard of you?"

John's lips twitched. "I guess you could say we step in to even the score and help the underdog."

She nodded and glanced around the nondescript office noticing not even a picture hung on the white walls. A row of windows was covered by lowered blinds for privacy. A long conference table ran the length of the room, yet there was no other indication to suggest what he'd told her was true.

"Looks like the underdogs pay very well for your services."

"I've already told you, we're the good guys. We help whoever needs us, no matter how big their bank account." He shook his head as if dismissing the conversation. "Let's get back to your problem."

"I don't have a problem besides you owning the knife."

His face remained blank, his stare hard. "Truth time, Delaney. Why do those people keep trying to kill you? And how does the Wellborn dagger fit into it?"

She leaned back in her chair and crossed her legs. His gaze followed the movement and she grinned. He wasn't just good looking. No, that title didn't do him justice. John was hot with a capital H, and, unfortunately, everything about him was her type. Tall, dark, handsome, with dimples she wanted to kiss and a body that could rock her world. The depths of his ocean blue eyes were reeling her in, almost demanding her to tell him her secrets. The fact that he was almost drooling was a bonus. She wondered what he liked best about her. Was he a leg man or did he prefer the breast? She grinned at the thought of finding out. She shook the thought from her mind. No man was worth the heartache he could cause. She knew first-hand. No. She'd be better keeping this professional, if that was all it was. "Since you know which era the dagger is from, I assume you know the significance."

His face remained unreadable, if you didn't count the heat in his eyes. Heat for her? Heat for the answers? Or heat for the daggers? Did he even know there were two?

"I've heard the story. But it's just a myth."

Delaney shrugged, knowing full well the history of the piece and the new meaning it would bring to her future. "Then you won't mind parting with it."

His pulled the box out of his jacket and set it on the table, pushing it closer to her. "I won't be parting with it, but I did promise you a closer look." He slid the knife across the table. "This is your chance."

Delaney slowly opened the box like she would a Christmas present she wanted to savor. Her heart raced and fingers tingled at the thrill of finally getting her hands on the dagger and performing the up-close-and-personal examination she'd only dreamed of. She wasn't after the dagger for the superstition associated with it but because of the murder that it had been used in. This was her way out.

She picked it up from the bed of satin it was housed inside and ran her finger down the blade before examining the handle. "Exquisite, isn't it?"

She didn't wait for a reply. "The Wellborns were known for their remarkable craftsmanship." She ran her fingers over the rubies studding the handle. "And the rubies, although small, have clarity unlike any others. It's amazing that the knife resurfaced, much less ended up in a pawn shop."

She flipped the knife over in her hand before glancing up. "You know the tale of Princess Mya and how she saved the Prince?"

John grinned. "The only princess in history who didn't need saving but ended up saving the guy's ass."

"The only *recorded* princess in history," Delaney corrected and then chuckled. "But do you know the story about how she came to have the knife?"

John leaned forward, crossing his arms on the table. "The witch." His lips quirked. "Not many people know that."

Delaney nodded and lifted the knife so she could get a closer look at the hilt. No initials. Relief filled her and her shoulders relaxed. She'd found it. Thank God, she'd found the original. "It's said that the knife brings balance to the owner." Her thoughts turned back to the night her mother died. "Do you think it's possible?"

John remained silent. Had she crossed the line? Was John debating giving the guys in the white lab coats a call?

"I've read the old texts." John shrugged. "No one knows the name of the witch who forged it or what balance the texts are referring to." He slid the knife out of her hands and flipped it into the air before catching it by the handle. A parlor trick for her benefit? Was she supposed to be impressed?

Delaney took the knife back and grinned. "I do." She flipped the knife just as John had done and flung it toward the wall, the blade slicing through the air and embedding into the drywall, a move she'd learned while mastering her weapons class when getting her black belt. That little bit of information she'd keep to herself.

John rose and studied where the blade met drywall before glancing at her over his shoulder. She watched his lips twitch when he noticed the dead spider impaled on the tip.

He pulled the knife out in one fluid motion and pulled a handkerchief from his pocket. He wiped the blade down before securing it firmly back into the box. He replaced the lid and stuffed the box back into the pocket on the inside of his coat. "Supposing you do know and you had the knife, not to mention that the tale is actually true, what's the balance she's referring to?"

"I'm afraid that's private, Mr. Bennett."

"John," he corrected.

"John...It's still not your business."

A knock sounded on the door, and a tall, beautiful, blonde woman walked into the room. Was this the woman he was going to give the knife to? There was no question she was a drop-dead knockout. Delaney's stomach clenched. Had she read John wrong? Maybe he hadn't been as attracted to her as she'd originally thought.

"Hi." The woman handed John a file and sat down across from Delaney. "John, where are your manners?"

John flipped the file open and, without looking up, made the introductions. "Delaney Chance, this is my aunt, Claire Edwards. Aunt Claire, this is Delaney."

Ah...*Aunt* Claire.

"The one..."

John interrupted her. "Yes."

"The one what?" Delaney curiously questioned. Exactly what did John know about her? Maybe it was time she asked her own questions.

"The woman of his dreams, dear," Aunt Claire chimed in.

"More like nightmares," John mumbled before lifting his gaze. "Aunt Claire..." He shook his head to try and stifle the conversation.

She shrugged. "Well, it's true. Haven't you told her yet?"

John's head fell back on his shoulders and he clenched his eyes closed. Interesting.

"You've dreamt about me? Was that how you knew where I'd be, like a premonition or something?" Delaney asked, her lips tilting at the corners. Renewed butterflies erupted in her stomach and flitted around; it was as if she was the schoolgirl learning her first crush liked her. Just what the hell *had* she walked into?

The same guy, that John had called Uncle Butch, walked in carrying coffee cups. He set one down in front of Delaney and another in front of Claire before he leaned down and kissed her.

"Thank you, honey."

"Have you gotten her to talk yet?" The question was aimed at John while Butch stroked little circles on Claire's shoulder.

"*He*r is sitting right here. If there's something you'd like to know, just ask." Delaney harrumphed.

Claire chuckled and glanced up at her husband. "I like her already. So much spunk and attitude wrapped up in a cute little package."

John grinned and leaned back in his chair, his brow hitched. "Yeah, Uncle Butch, all you have to do is ask her."

Butch sat next to his wife, folding his big body into the tiny chair. The man was made of muscles and tattoos. He was handsome in a biker kind of way, and Claire was beautiful in a sleek and sophisticated fashion. They were opposites of the best kind. Delaney admired them both right from the start. Her yin to his yang.

Butch gave Delaney a mischievous grin before he asked, "Why don't we start with you telling me what the Jessup thugs want with you?"

Delaney's mouth parted. She'd known she would have to explain to John who those guys were, but she'd expected to buy a little bit more time to come up with a good story. One that didn't include the truth.

Claire sipped her coffee, and then one side of her mouth tilted up. The look on her face was one Delaney had seen on her mom, when she knew Delaney was fibbing.

Claire's brows rose, and then she smiled reassuringly.

Well crap. Delaney took a deep breath and met Butch's gaze. "I'm a reporter for *Chicago Daily*. I have reason to believe that Ritchie Jessup is responsible for several unsolved murders."

"Proof?" Butch questioned.

"An informant promised me proof. I'm not sure how the Jessups even found out I was working on the story. But I didn't get a chance to get the information before John here spooked him off."

"More like saved your ass, darling."

"I didn't need saving, Bennett."

John closed the file and looked at Delaney. Really looked at her for the first time since they'd met. His eyes caressed her face, even as the telltale signs of uncertainty crossed his features. His gaze held hers as if trying to read to her mind. "I don't like it. They are known killers and have been on the FBI's watch list for a long time. It's too dangerous. Does this have anything to do with the dagger?"

"The dagger is personal, and it's a good thing your opinion doesn't pay my bills. I'm only here because of my informant and to find the dagger." This time it was Delaney that let her gaze slide to his. "How is it you know who is on the FBI's watch list? That can't be public knowledge."

John smiled, but the answer didn't come from him. It came from Claire. "John's father is FBI and his mother is a forensic investigator with the Southall PD."

"Ah...must make for interesting dinner conversation," Delaney surmised.

A knock sounded on the door before two more men came into the room, carrying bags that looked oddly similar to her suitcase and backpack. "These were all she had in her room."

Delaney shoved back her seat and rose, staring pointedly at John. "Those are my things!"

John nodded. "Yes. They are."

"Who gave you permission to go into my hotel room?"

John stood, holding up his hands. "Listen, I just want to help and, with those thugs in town, it's safer if you stay someplace that has better security. The hotel isn't it."

"I never asked for your help. I've been fine on my own for the last five years and survived just fine. I. Don't. Need. Your. Help."

"Listen, doll, you may not need my help or want it, but you've got it. In my dreams, you're in trouble, and I don't want your disappearance on my conscience. So, if you won't stay with me, you have your choice of family members, each with fortresses that have the security of Fort Knox. Just consider us like extended family."

"Why...why would you go to all of this trouble?"

John's gaze never left her eyes. The tremulous color swirled in intensity. "You're the key."

"Excuse me?" she asked, hoping beyond anything that John was talking about something altogether different than the truth and reality as she knew it to be. "What key?"

"You're the constant in my dreams and, if I don't help you, I can't move on with my own life. I tried to ignore the calling before and it almost killed me. I won't let your stubbornness get in the way of fixing whatever problems you've got."

"Screw you, John Bennett."

Delaney marched over to where her suitcase and backpack lay. She threw the sack over her shoulder, grabbed the handle, and started heading for the door. She'd find her own way out of this psychotic place, even if she had to walk ten miles back to civilization. No bastard was going to call her stubborn. No asshole would live to tell about it. If she had that damn knife, she'd toss it directly at his heartless chest.

"Now, dear," Claire said, meeting her by the door. "My nephew is a little rough around the edges but he means well. Honest." Claire took the handle on the suitcase. "Butch and I would be happy to have you as our guest. You can come and go as you please, and we'll all sleep a little better knowing that you're safe." Claire patted Delaney on the arm. "How does that sound?"

Delaney chewed her bottom lip between her teeth as she debated the request. She knew the Jessup gang wouldn't give up until she was dead, and the fact that they'd found her and she'd yet to meet her informant and yet to obtain the knife was slowing down her schedule. A little extra security couldn't hurt, as long as it wasn't *him.*

Claire grinned and clapped her hands. "Perfect, it's settled."

Delaney's brows dipped. "I didn't say yes."

Claire's grin slipped. "Oh...I'm sorry, Delaney. Home-cooked meals come with the arrangements, if that helps entice you."

Delaney met John's gaze once more. His arms were crossed over his chest and his stance read defiance. She grinned. "Yes, Claire. I'd love to stay. Thank you."

John threw his hands up in defeat. "That wasn't the plan, Aunt Claire."

"It is now, John, unless you'd like a dagger through the heart."

Before Delaney could question the statement, Claire was pulling her out the door and waving off the guards trying to stop her. She walked through the premises and led Delaney to a house just across the estate. Claire walked through the house as though she owned it. Maybe she did. Maybe Delaney had been the one who was played.

CHAPTER 4

John grunted as he carried Delaney's suitcase upstairs, to one of the spare bedrooms, for his Aunt Claire. Delaney may have thought she'd avoided having to deal with John, but she was mistaken. John grinned as he walked past the room that he liked to frequent when staying overnight for Claire's parties. Yeah...that room was about to be used again. He chuckled as he tossed Delaney's suitcase and backpack onto the bed in the adjoining room.

Movement out the window, on the lawn below, had him moving to the other side of the room. He lifted the sheer curtains and studied the women below. Seemed Aunt Claire was giving Delaney a tour of the grounds. His dreams had been invaded, just like his family. What the hell was going on with this girl, and why wouldn't his subconscious just let him forget? John entered the adjoining guest room where he liked to stay. Aunt Claire wouldn't mind…maybe.

John took inventory of the spare clothes and toiletries he'd left behind to make sure he had enough. There was no telling where Delaney might try to go if he left her completely alone. No, it was better he stuck close by, better to keep an eye on her, and better to make sure his family didn't tell the little reporter about their gifts. That was the last thing they needed. Exposure like that would force them all into hiding and had the possibility to ruin careers. The quicker he got the little woman out of his hair and moving on, the better for all involved. John pulled the dagger box out of his jacket before tossing the coat onto the bed. "So…this little baby was what she was after."

He shook his head. What a shame. He wasn't parting with it and, if he had read the defiance in her eyes correctly, she wasn't leaving without it. John took the dagger out of the box and glanced around the room. He needed a place where she wouldn't find it. A place she wouldn't look. He grinned as he remembered the hiding spot that his mom talked about when he was a child. He moved over to the bookshelf and ran his finger along the spines until he found the book he wanted. Not wanted, but needed, he corrected; he'd win this little game of hide and seek. The embossed words

War and Peace stared back at him. "Perfect and appropriate."

He opened the hollowed-out book, stuck the dagger inside, and left the now empty knife box in his sock drawer under his boxers. She'd really have to go snooping to find the box, and then she was going to be pissed that the box was empty when she realized what he'd done. Hell, maybe she'd surprise him and not look at all.

He chuckled and shook his head. He wouldn't bet on it.

John trotted back downstairs and followed the smell of coffee into the kitchen. Laughter and conversation filled the normally quiet house. He stepped inside the door and paused.

Aunt Claire was flipping through pages, pointing people out.

Heat infused his cheeks and his body tensed. "Tell me you didn't."

Both Aunt Claire and Delaney glanced up from the photo album and grinned. "Just showing her a couple pictures of the family, just in case she meets them."

Delaney's grin grew bigger. "You were a cute kid, Bennett."

"John," he reminded her.

"You were a cute kid, John Bennett," she teased back.

"Don't be so quick to compliment me, Delaney Chance. I put you in the spare room right next to mine, and we have an adjoining door and bathroom." He wiggled his brows. "You know...in case you get scared of the dark and all."

That comment got him a heated glare from Delaney that threatened retribution. Aunt Claire cleared her throat and clapped her hands. "Perfect. I'll tell the staff we have guests while you show her to her room, and then we'll work on a game plan to get her settled and out of this dreaded mess."

Delaney stood. "Mrs. Edwards, please don't go to all the trouble. I won't be here long enough to get in your way."

"Oh, Delaney, you can call me Claire, and you're welcome to stay as long as you'd like. We have state-of-the-art security, not to mention my husband is one of the best in the business, and John here—"

"That's enough, Aunt Claire. You don't need to overwhelm her with any more stories about me."

The less she knows the better, until we know who she is. John repeated the saying over and over in his head in hopes that his aunt would read his thoughts.

Aunt Claire gave a slight nod. Yep, she had read his mind. He was certain of it when she raised her brows and placed a fake smile on her face. "Yes...well, let's get you settled."

John gestured back out the way he'd entered. "After you, Delaney."

Delaney glanced back and forth between John and his aunt before she walked out of the kitchen and let John lead her to her room. He held the door open. "Welcome to your new accommodations."

Delaney stepped inside and ran her hand over the bedspread before turning back to John. "You know this is unnecessary. I'm sure the Jessups think I skipped town by now and they'll go back to whatever hole they climbed out of."

John slowly closed the distance between them until he was standing in front of her. His gaze fell to her lips before meeting her eyes. Damn, this woman was beautiful. He wouldn't touch her; he wouldn't kiss her; he wouldn't break whatever trust he was earning. Not now, not when he was just figuring out what secrets she held.

Delaney's tongue slipped out and slid across her red lips as she held his heated gaze. "John."

"Hmm?" The little minx was playing. The right thing to do was to step back, move out of her personal space, but his feet were frozen in place. He'd dreamed about Delaney in his bed and in his arms, not that he'd shared that information with his family.

"The dagger...Is it for your girlfriend?" Her voice sounded seductive, barely above a whisper. The kind he'd expect to be accompanied by sweet nothings in his ear.

"No girlfriend." He wasn't about to reveal whom it was for. He wouldn't give Delaney another victim for her sob story.

"Good." She reached up, laid her hand on his neck, and pulled him down until her lips meshed with his. All rational though fled his brain as he pulled her soft body against his, holding her, caressing her, enjoying and savoring what she offered. Damn, this woman could kiss. She nibbled his bottom lip until he opened, and then she took and tasted and moaned, sinking farther into his hold. He knew it wasn't right, that what she was doing was strictly for the dagger, but he couldn't pull away. Her heated body pressed against his, her lips, her tongue, and her caresses all seemed driven by desire, a desire he shared. This was literally the woman of his dreams. And yet, he knew he had to let her go, even the playing field so she'd understand the kiss wouldn't garner the prize she sought. She wanted the dagger and he wouldn't let that happen. Not in this lifetime.

John broke the kiss and stepped back, instantly missing the heat from her body and her lips. "Delaney...if you're only doing this for the dagger..."

"Screw you, Bennett." The slap came quick and hard. His cheek stung, but he wouldn't give her the satisfaction of showing it. He'd expected to see disappointment in her eyes, but he was met with a burning fire instead.

"You wish, doll."

Delaney wasn't as fast this time. He caught her open palm in mid-air. This was getting out of hand; had his mother, father, or hell, even Aunt Claire watched their exchange, they'd disown him on the spot. John brought her hand up to his mouth and kissed her open palm. "I'm sorry. I don't know you well enough to know what your motives are."

"Damn right, you don't." Delaney yanked her hand from him and propped her fists on her hips. "Did it ever occur to you that I kissed you for no other reason than I wanted to?"

"Did you?"

"It doesn't matter. You don't have to worry about it happening again."

Just where in the hell did she think she was going? John smiled. Did she know how long the walk into town was?

John rubbed his hands over his face and used the adjoining door to go into his room and plop down on his bed. She needed time to cool off. And he needed the same, but for a completely different reason. She'd set his blood boiling, but not in the same way as hers. That kiss had ramped his libido into overdrive. Was she playing him? He closed his eyes and replayed every moment since they'd met. She was an actress; she'd proven that from the start. Her goal was the dagger. She'd come clean about it, but only when pressed. First thing first was the Jessup gang. They were killers, and they'd stop at nothing to get what they wanted. John opened his eyes and let out a deep breath as he pushed up from the bed. He needed his weapon and, on top of that, he needed details from the team that was following the Jessups everywhere they went, discovering everyone they called. It was going to be a full-scale operation. He was going to need his Uncle Jake's help and a lot of it.

John pulled the semiautomatic out from where it was nestled in his leg holster. He checked the clip and shoved it back in. He had one goal—save Delaney—and he wasn't going to get anything done by trying to figure out everything in his head. He grabbed his coat and headed down the stairs to find Aunt Claire standing at the open door, leaning on the frame. "What are you doing, Aunt Claire?"

She glanced over her shoulder before turning again to watch the driveway. "She left."

"She what?" John quickly pushed by his aunt and out onto the porch. "Why didn't you stop her?"

"John," Aunt Claire said as she moved to his side and slid her palm around his arm, "I read her mind. She's still pissed and I can't say I blame her."

John spun around on his aunt and pointed down the driveway. "There are people after her and you let her leave...by herself. Are you crazy?"

Claire clasped her hands in front of her. "Are you done?"

John lowered his gaze to his feet. "I apologized, Aunt Claire."

"I know, I read that too. Her thoughts were a jumbled mess. She wanted to trust you, but she kept debating how smart that idea might be. I'd say you royally screwed up, kid."

Knowing he was being an ass, John lowered his head, clenching his eyes closed. "I'm sorry. It seems being a jerk has become second nature for me since she arrived."

"I would say so."

He looked up. "But how could you let her leave when you knew she was in trouble?"

"That's easy, dear. Butch drove her and promised to look out for her."

John released the breath he didn't realize he was holding. "Thank you. Thank you. Thank you." He kissed her cheek. "I'll call him from the SUV."

He hopped down the stairs leading to the driveway and skidded to a stop.

"John, did you forget something?"

"I didn't drive here. Can I borrow your car?"

She pulled the keys from her pocket and tossed them to him. "I figured you might ask. Now go get your girl and play nice. You might have a bit of groveling to do but it will make you humble."

John grinned. His family knew him well. "I'll do my best."

He slid behind the wheel and started down the drive as he hit his Bluetooth. His uncle answered on the first ring. "Uncle Butch."

"About time. I'm sitting outside Emma's café and I've got eyes inside and on the security. She's fine. She's on her second cup of coffee though."

"I'm on my way. I'll take over when I get there."

"You better hurry, kid. Dustin George just slid into her booth, and you know how smooth that guy can be."

"Thanks." John disconnected the call. Dustin was a lady's man. He knew the right things to say, the right things to do. He used women; he'd use her and, when he was done, he'd toss her to the side and start hunting his next target. There wasn't a chance in hell that Delaney would fall for him. She was smarter than that. She was smarter than he'd given her credit for. The passion in their shared kiss had set his body on fire. He hadn't expected it, and he definitely hadn't wanted it to stop. No, Dustin George wouldn't be honing in on John's territory. John had the one thing that Delaney wanted most in town, and it wasn't a roll between the sheets. He had the dagger; he had the security to protect her; and she had the one thing that he wanted back more than anything, his sanity.

John pushed down harder on the accelerator. His mind replayed the last time he'd been in Emma's with Delaney. The woman had a death wish, returning to where the Jessups had found her. Had she lost her mind? John turned down Main Street. Apprehension filled his gut. Would she even hear him out? He'd already apologized; she should have just accepted it and let it go. Why did women dwell on the drama? He accepted he was wrong and tried to make it right. It should be a done deal. They should have already moved past that situation. He pulled up and parked along the street behind his uncle. John tapped on the window and waited for Butch to lower the glass.

"She's still inside but Dustin hasn't moved an inch. Actually, he just got a second cup of coffee, but the good news for you is that she looks bored out of her mind."

"Really?"

"Yep. We've got eyes watching the cameras and a team nearby. Let me know if you need anything else. I'm going to check in with the team we put on the Jessups to make sure they aren't in route from the hotel."

"I'd appreciate that." John tapped on the top of the SUV. "I'll see you back at the house."

"Hey, kid." Butch paused while putting the SUV in drive. "She's a woman. She's going to be stubborn and give you attitude like your aunts did to all of us, but remember...if you play your cards right, she could be worth it."

"Uh, yeah...I'll keep that in mind."

Delaney Chance wasn't going to be sticking around long enough for him to really get to know. But the longer she stayed in town, the more time he'd be spending with her. He needed her trust more than anything else if he had any hope of eradicating her from his dreams and his life. His dream job was calling.

John rubbed the scar on his side as he remembered how he'd come to have it. He'd been out running one night. An image of had Delaney popped into his mind, and he'd slowed to a walk, unaware of his surroundings. The mugger appeared out of nowhere and they'd fought. The knife shoved in his side had miraculously missed every major organ. Getting his command leaders not to call in his family had been hard, but he'd managed, knowing that if they'd heard, they'd all show up and take over the way they normally would.

His Aunt Emma had called when her radar had indicated one of them was in trouble but he'd managed to convince her that it wasn't him. He'd needed time to digest what had happened. Time to figure out what he wanted to do about his life, and he'd hoped to lay low while figuring out how to get her out of his mind.

****

Delaney purchased her coffee and sat at the same booth in the back of the room where she'd been earlier that day. It was a risk coming back to the coffee shop where the Jessups had found her last time, but it was a risk she was willing to take. She needed some alone time to figure out her next move. John had her dagger, but where in the hell would her mom have hidden the evidence she needed? Her informant had told her he knew where the photo was stashed. He was supposed to take her to it. She sent him a text to tell him where to meet her.

She glanced out the window and spotted the SUV with John's uncle sitting inside. She was glad he had followed and was keeping his distance. The move was smart and inconspicuous. A blonde woman, that Delaney didn't recognize, walked by the table and laid down a napkin before hurrying outside.

Delaney picked it up and read the words. *I'm watching you.* The napkin was signed *Marco.* Her gaze went out the window, trying to find where the woman had disappeared, but the streets were riddled with people walking by, and none of them were her. Delaney's mind started to race with the implications. If he got to her before she got the proof, she was as good as dead. Her gaze landed on John's uncle. He had the phone pressed to his ear. She was so preoccupied she'd missed the new man who'd slid into the seat opposite her.

"Hi, beautiful, I'm Dustin."

Delaney let out a lengthy sigh. She was used to getting hit on, but she was in no mood for the company of a complete stranger. "I'm waiting for someone."

"Great." He took a sip of his coffee. "I'll keep you company until he arrives."

"Oh, that isn't necessary."

"It's called southern hospitality."

Delaney sat there and listened to Dustin talk all about the town and himself. He'd barely let her get a word in edgewise when she spotted John about to walk in. She grinned.

****

John took a deep breath and walked into the café. He headed toward the counter where the ladies gave him his usual. He turned and scanned the room until his gaze met hers and held it. Should he stay or should he go? He debated the pros and cons of each choice when the decision was taken out of his hands. She motioned him over and John didn't know what to expect. He'd barely made it to the table when she held out her hand. "Sweetie, you're late."

He glanced at his watch as he slid into the booth next to her. "I'm sorry for making you wait, baby."

John laid his arm across the back of the booth and turned toward Dustin. "Thanks for keeping my girl company, Dustin, but if you'll excuse us, we have some plans to make."

Dustin's glare was fleeting until Delaney returned her gaze to him. "You shouldn't leave such a smart, beautiful lady waiting, Bennett. She might realize she deserves better."

"She already knows she deserves better, don't you, babe?"

Delaney grinned. "Damn right I do."

She laced her fingers behind John's head and pulled him down for an encore of the kiss they'd shared in the room. They forgot any bystanders as their tongues dueled in the same dance he remembered. She lingered and he felt a smile cross her lips when she pulled back.

"I'm just glad you showed at all," she whispered against his lips before turning back to Dustin. "He's a god in the sack, passionate and caring, every woman's dream."

John tilted his head back and laughed, no longer able to hold it in.

Delaney snuggled into John's side. "Now if you'll excuse us, Dustin, I have plans to seduce him into taking me back to bed, and I wasn't expecting an audience."

Dustin frowned as he slid out of the booth. "I'll just leave you to it." He dropped his business card on the table. "It was a pleasure, Delaney. Call me when you come to your senses and dump Bennett." He gave them both a sly grin. "If you're half as smart as he said you are...you will."

John's muscles bunched. The only thing keeping him in the booth was Delaney's hand on his thigh. He wouldn't risk her moving it; otherwise, he would have jumped up and knocked the shit out of this little fucker.

"Oh, Dustin," Delaney called as he turned to leave. Her eyes sparkled with mischief. "He gives me multiple orgasms that make me pass out from pleasure. On top of that, he's sexy and brilliant and can outshoot me with not only a nine-millimeter but a semiautomatic. And yet, he's got enough class not to boast about it. So don't hold your breath waiting for me, sugar, because he's more than man enough to keep me satisfied in bed and out." She wiggled her fingers. "Bye bye now."

"That was epic, Ms. Chance, but now I'm afraid you owe me one."

Delaney glanced up and grinned. "Look around, Bennett. I just made you a legend. I think that makes us even."

John glanced around the café to find all of the women staring. A woman easily ten years his senior winked and blew him a kiss.

Leaning into her side, he whispered, "Let's get out of here. Do you want to take a walk?"

She nodded, downed the rest of her coffee, and slid out of the booth behind him. She grabbed his hand and positioned his arm around her shoulders, still linking their fingers together. She was good, an actress, he reminded himself.

"Let's go, stud."

John pulled the door open and they stepped out onto the street. "I didn't peg you for a princess that needed saving."

She released his hand. "I'm not. That display wasn't for my benefit. I could have told the jerk to buzz off. I was waiting for you." She glanced up at him. "What took you so long?"

Remarkable, funny, and delusional. Those are the words he'd pick to describe Delaney Chance.

She'd removed her hand from his, but he hadn't dropped his hold on her shoulder. He maneuvered her into the alley between two buildings and then dropped the charade. "Okay, what gives? One minute you're slapping me for suggesting you had less-than-honest intentions for the kiss, then you leave all pissy, and now you're acting crazy. Is this normal behavior for you? Have you seen a doctor for the multiple personalities you're displaying?"

Delaney leaned back against the brick building and chuckled. "Bennett, I said you were smart. Don't prove me wrong."

"Ouch. This is your opportunity to come clean, Delaney. What aren't you telling me?"

"You know why I'm here. You know what I want."

If only that were the case. "You want the dagger."

She tilted her head from side to side. "Yes and no."

"What the hell does that mean?"

"Yes, I want the dagger but, no, that isn't the only reason I'm here."

"Explain."

"I still have to meet my informant for the proof I need." She glanced up at him, her lips quirked. "Do you always dream about me?"

The question threw him off guard. How was he supposed to answer that without giving away his own secrets? He didn't trust her enough to tell her the truth. Not yet.

"No, just for the last few weeks, and it's always the same thing—the alley, the pawnshop, and you in trouble. I don't know why it keeps happening but I'm supposed to help you, Delaney."

"Why do you suppose that is?"

"I don't know."

"Well, I guess we shouldn't screw with fate or whatever the hell is going on." She sidestepped around him and started back toward Main Street, calling over her shoulder, "Well, are you coming?"

She slowed at the end of the alley, glancing both ways as if looking for something while waiting for him to catch up.

"Where are we going?"

Delaney's beautiful green eyes sparkled with mischief. "I hear there's a lake somewhere around here."

John led her back to Aunt Claire's car and held the passenger door open for her. "It used to be my favorite place to go."

She slid into the seat and was buckling her belt by the time he got in on the driver's side. "Will you take me?"

"Sure. I'll show you around." He glanced at her. "Then we'll go back to Aunt Claire's for dinner."

Delaney was nervous, her gaze darting around and taking in everything they passed. She glanced behind them several times before she settled into her seat.

"I'm not going to let anything happen to you."

"Hmm," she said as though she didn't believe him.

Delaney was a conundrum, confusing him at every turn. The kiss, the slap, and then there was what she'd done in the café. Just who was this woman? Was his dream really   a   nightmare?

CHAPTER 5

Delaney listened with intent as John showed her around the lake, pointing out the places and things that clearly mattered most to him. He slowed, tossing the car into park when they reached an old looking cabin that had seen better days. They got out of the car and she moved to stand next to him, the proximity making her feel safe and yet uncertain. He stood in silence, his eyes focused and his lips turned down at the corners. What was he thinking? She glanced at the cabin and studied it alongside him. "It's kind of old," she remarked. "Is this your family's?"

"No." John's brows dipped before he shook off whatever he'd been thinking and spun around, heading toward the water.

"Hey..." She caught up with him and glanced back at the wooden structure. "You okay?"

"My Aunt Emma almost died in that cabin," he said quietly while reaching down to pick up a rock at his feet. He skipped it across the lake's glassy surface, causing ripples along its path.

She touched his arm. "We can leave if you'd like. I've seen enough."

Her mission, to get far away from the center of town and prying eyes, had served her purpose. She'd liked being surrounded by the calming water of a lake growing up. Her mother would take her once in a blue moon, but she could still recall those times as some of the best in her life.

John laid his arm around her shoulders and steered her along the shoreline. "I promised to show you around, and I don't ever go back on my word."

They walked in contemplative silence until they reached a small dock. "I grew up on this water. My mom taught me to swim here." The wood beneath his boots creaked as they walked along the planks to the end. "I had my first beer here." John chuckled. "I was your typical teenage punk." His brows lifted and a sly smile split his lips. "I lost my virginity here, too."

"I bet you were a stud back in the day. You had your pick of all of the girls, didn't you?"

He gestured back the way they'd come. "Nah, I was too shy. I was the quiet guy who got good grades." He glanced down at her, giving her a view of one of his dimples. "And we both know the nerd doesn't get the girl."

"Well, you got the attention of at least one."

John's lips split into a grin. "Gretchen Filcraft."

"Did you date long?"

"Nope, I had a major crush on her, but she was only using me."

"For what?"

"To lose her virginity before going off to college."

Delaney bumped his shoulder. "It was her loss. I guess she never saw the movie where the nerd shows up to the reunion loaded with millions and women hanging on his arm." She let her gaze travel down his body before meeting his eyes. "Looks like they'll be wishing they were nicer to you."

"So, you like what you see?" John teased and tossed his arm around her shoulders like they'd been friends for a long time instead of less than a day.

"You aren't bad looking, Bennett." She glanced up at him. "But my stamp of approval doesn't matter; it's always been missing the glue on the back to hold it in place. Now,"—she smiled—"as the owner of the dagger and someone who appreciates the piece as much as I do, that raises my personal opinion of you to a whole new level. You've got brains to match your brawn." Delaney shrugged and teased, "Who knew?"

He pulled her car door open and waited for her to slide in. "You haven't seen anything yet."

And that's what she was afraid of. The guy was already getting under her skin. Funny, smart, and sexy as hell, but he had one major flaw in her book. He wasn't giving her the dagger. She'd end up doing the same thing her mother had done almost two decades ago. She'd steal the bitch back. It was ironic that she'd be using it only as insurance, the same reason her mother had all those years ago.

He shut the door and moved around to the driver's side. While starting his engine, John's cell phone rang. He held it to his ear. "Bennett."

He hooked his seatbelt.

"Yes, Aunt Claire. We'll pick it up on the way." He disconnected the call. "We're on dessert duty. The bakery is expecting us."

The request was something she would have expected her mother to make years ago. The similarities between John's aunt and her own mother were pretty startling. They didn't look alike, but they were both sophisticated and carried themselves with dignity and grace. Delaney propped her head against the window and watched the scenery pass by. Her thoughts shifted back to the fateful night when her life had changed forever. Everything she'd done had been for her mother, and she wouldn't stop until she'd completed her last dying wish. The dagger was within reach and, no matter how good looking, smart and savvy John Bennett was, he would not be the one to stop her from finishing what her mother had lacked the courage to so while she was alive . Not now, not ever.

John turned down Main Street and parked in front of the bakery. "This will only take a second if you want to wait here."

She smiled. "Sure."

Through the large glass window, she watched the people milling around inside. Some people were sitting at the tables eating desserts. Others, with to-go bags, sniffed the contents with grins on their faces as they left the store. With every step John tried to take to the counter, a woman stepped in his way. She didn't have to read lips to know they were hitting on him. What she'd said in the café must have made its rounds rather quickly. John turned back to look at her, his brows creased, his eyes sending out a silent plea for help.

"Poor guy."

She'd stepped out of the car and closed the door when a hand landed on her shoulder. A large body pressed into her back. The faint smell of cigarettes drifted up to her nose. They'd found her.

"Where's your source?" Ritchie Jessup's right-hand man, Marco, demanded in her ear.

"He isn't here." Delaney tightened the hold on her purse straps. "He backed out. I have nothing."

He pressed an object into the small of her back. "I don't believe you, Del."

Delaney swallowed around the knot in her throat. "I don't care what you believe. It's the truth."

His other arm came around her waist, holding her body tight until she could barely draw a breath. "Give me the dagger and the photo, and you can come back to your dad." He pressed his erection into her backside and ran his tongue up her cheek, leaving a wet trail on her skin. "He promised I could have you."

Bile rose to her throat. Ritchie didn't own her, and there was no way in hell she'd let Marco get close to her again.

"He doesn't own me and you're nothing more than his little lapdog."

"I'll show you, b—"

He clamped his mouth shut when John walked out of the bakery, surprising not only Marco, but Delaney as well. A gun was pointed at the thug holding her captive.

"Put your hands where I can see them."

Marco tightened his hold. "I don't think so." He leaned into Delaney, whispering in her ear. "Who's he supposed to be, some type of knight in shining armor? Richie isn't going to like this, sugar. You just signed this guy's death warrant."

Marco released his hold on Delaney and shoved his gun beneath his leather jacket. John kept his gun trained on the asshole, while reaching for Delaney with his other hand, yanking her to his side and then shoving her behind him.

Marco raised his hands in the air, showing John he wasn't armed. "This isn't over, kid. I'll be seeing you around. You can count on it."

Marco disappeared into the alley between the buildings as quickly as he'd shown up. That wouldn't be the last they'd see of him. Not now, not ever. John grabbed her hand in a sure grip, ushering her into the car. Seconds later he was in the driver's side and they were speeding down the road. Before they even turned the corner, the Bluetooth in the car rang.

"Bennett," John answered through gritted teeth.

"John." An unfamiliar woman's voice echoed through the car. "Where are you?"

John let out a breath. "Hey, Aunt Em. Delaney and I are fine and on our way to Aunt Claire's house." John glanced in

Delaney's direction. "Can you let her know that the chocolate cake wasn't ready?"

"Sure, I'll tell her. I just wanted to give you a heads-up. I just got off the phone with your mom. She was worried about the cake too. I'd suggest you call her when you get to Claire's. Sorry about that."

"No problem, thanks for checking on us, Aunt Em. I'll call if I have any more problems."

****

"Your family sure likes their dessert."

"They sure do." John breathed a sigh of relief as he loosened his hold on the wheel. When he'd heard his Aunt Emma's voice, he immediately knew the reason for the call. Her PMS-like radar was going off, telling her that one of the family members was in trouble. She was probably doubled over in cramps while grilling Momma Mae. The cramps were her sign that something wasn't right, her own personal hell of a gift that she had to live with. With the constant troubles that plagued his family, it was no wonder that Aunt Em was the first to realize something was wrong.

The cake wasn't chocolate like he'd suggested. It was lemon, but there was no way he could have used that word. Those were two of the four code words that his aunts had come up with long ago to help diffuse other's hearing and understanding Emma's questioning concerns. Each served its own purpose, each a warning or an answer to indicate the level of threat they were under. Chocolate was the easiest for his aunts to remember, the meaning simple. They were fine, but couldn't talk. Lemons, well, that was another story. If he uttered that word, it would call in the cavalry with guns blaring. Pecan meant fine but stay away and the dreaded word broccoli meant head for the safe house because all hell was breaking loose.

Neither John nor Delaney spoke another word the entire ride back to the compound. She sat in her seat with a firm grasp on her pendant. Thick tension filled the car and matched his mood. Of all the problems in the entire world, the one person who needed his help was running from someone on the FBI's watch list. Not only that, but it appeared his little dream wrecker was personal with Ritchie Jessup and his second in command. John had seen the FBI's list. He'd studied it while in training. These guys were scum and, worse than that, they were killers.

John parked the car but didn't move to get out. "Is there something you need to tell me, Delaney?"

He turned to measure her response.

"Yeah..." She faltered in the silence that surrounded them. "I think you should leave town for a while, at least until I find what

I'm looking for. It will be safer for you that way."

A swift, hot anger clenched his gut. This woman didn't know shit about him; she hadn't a clue what he was capable of. "Don't worry about me, princess. I need to know how well you know Ritchie Jessup and Marco. I need to understand your association with them now that I've brought my family into this mess."

She sat motionless and silent, as if mulling over her answer.

"Delaney, I need to know."

She met his gaze, her body stiff and unyielding, as though he had struck her. Her fingers clutched the door handle. "I'm sorry I brought you into this. At least it isn't too late for me to fix my mistake."

She jumped from the car and went running into the house. He was only a second behind and hot on her heels. She wasn't getting away from him, not now. He had resigned himself, when his dreams started, that he would be the one to help her, and he had every intention of doing so.

John had cleared the door and was headed for the stairs when Butch caught his arm.

"What's going on?" Butch demanded. "First, Emma called and then your mother, and then they brought up the chocolate cake. Everything was fine when I left you. What the hell happened?"

John glanced up the stairs. "I'm sorry, Uncle Butch, but this conversation is going to have to wait. She's about to leave and I have to stop her before she ends up getting herself killed."

Butch dropped his hold and John took the steps two at a time. When he'd reached the landing, Butch hollered after him, "Your mother is on her way and, if I know your mom, she's bringing her own arsenal with her."

John skidded in his tracks. "Stall her." He held up his hands. "Tell her I'm okay, but stall her for as long as you can." He glanced over his shoulder and down the hall, where he could hear Delaney moving around. "I have to take care of this."

"You know how she can get when she's on a mission, but I'll see what I can do."

John headed Butch's warning and headed directly for Delaney's guest room. He pushed the door open, with more force than needed, startling Delany in her quest. She had her suitcase opened and was looking around the room in a frantic search.

"Where's my backpack?" she asked in a high-pitched voice. "I know you brought it up here."

John leaned against the doorframe. "Delaney, just calm down and let's discuss this. You don't have to worry about what those men will do to me. I can handle myself."

She dropped to her knees and crouched down to see under the bed, pushing her hair out of her eyes when she resurfaced. "I'm sure you can, Bennett, but you're right. He's dangerous, and I'm the reason he's in town."

"John," he corrected her. "So that's it. You're just going to leave?" John crossed his arms over his chest. "Just like that? What about the dagger?"

That question stopped her frantic search. She rose from her crouch, meeting his gaze.

"Tell me how you're connected to Jessup."

"Give me the dagger."

He shook his head. "Sorry, can't do that." He paused, his voice strained when he continued. "Were you sleeping with him? Is he your boyfriend?"

Delaney's mouth dropped open as her chest heaved. Fire sparked in her eyes and, if he wasn't mistaken, her face was turning a bit red as she clenched her fist by her side. "It's none of your business, Bennett."

Oh, the little princess had a temper to match her spunk. There was no way this side of her was an act. No, he was reading her like a textbook, and he knew exactly which buttons to push.

He stalked to her, and his palm cupped her reddening cheek. "That's where you're wrong. If I had to guess, Jessup is already on his way. If I'm about to fight this guy, I should at least know why."

He leaned down, making himself eye level with her, wanting to make sure she understood. "I gave you my word that I wouldn't let anything happen to you. I don't ever go back on my word."

Her soft hand covered his.

"You don't understand." Her voice came out a whisper. "I'm sorry it has to be this way, Bennett."

She dropped her hand and reared back; he caught a glimpse of her right hook before it landed against his face. The unexpected blow swiveled his body to the side and knocked him to the ground. His head hit the carpet and that was the last he remembered.

****

He felt gentle hands on his cheeks before he heard his mom's voice. "Are you okay, baby?"

John shot up into a sitting position, the room spinning in his gaze. He grabbed his throbbing cheek. "Where is she?"

"She's down in the library. We talked her out of leaving." His mom grinned. "I'm sure it had nothing to do with your dad threatening to haul her into the FBI offices for questioning. I guess you ignored her mom's warning and underestimated her right hook, huh?"

"Yeah, you can say that." Realization slapped him in the face. If she'd been left with his dad, he'd start the interrogation. He was one man who wouldn't let anyone screw with his family, none of his relatives would. She was probably shaking like a scared little kitten and, God forbid, Uncle Mike or Uncle Butch joined the tag team for information. Delaney didn't stand a chance. His throbbing cheek momentarily forgotten, his worry for Delaney kicked into overdrive. He grabbed his mom's hand and pulled himself off the floor.

"This woman is going to be the death of me."

His mom chuckled. "I'm sure she's ready for you to save her from your father and Uncle Mike about now."

John squeezed his mother's hand. "Thanks, Mom. The Jessups are after her and have now threatened me. I think it might be best if dad and you go to the beach house for a while and take Dixon and the aunts with you."

Abby gave him a crooked smile. "Uh….how about no? Absolutely not."

"Mom…I'm not a kid anymore. I can take care of myself."

Abby cupped his hurt cheek and turned his head to get a better look at the side of his face. "Yeah, I can tell. If it's all the same, I think your dad and I will stick around for this one."

John followed his mom out of the room and down the stairs toward the library. His mom opened the door and paused, stopping John in his tracks.

"What in the world?" Abby whispered, and her hand landed on the gun in her belt. Her knee-jerk reaction was to reach for her weapon.

Delaney had Uncle Mike around the throat with her arm and his hand bent in an unnatural position behind his back.

Her eyes were wet, her face stained with tears. "That's far enough. All I wanted to do was leave. I don't want to hurt anyone."

Heat licked John's face as his imagination ran wild with what she'd been through to make her cry. He knew his dad and uncle. They might have been demanding, but the proof was in her tears. Or was it? "Delaney, he's not getting enough air. Let him go."

Mike had his big, beefy hands curled around her arm, trying to keep her from killing him.

John lifted his hands and took a tentative step into the room. "Come on, Delaney, let him go. I'll take you wherever you want to go."

He moved to his dad's side, placed his palm over his dad's Glock, and lowered it to the floor.

His mom's cell phone rang, but she didn't make a move to answer it.

The house phone rang next and was picked up on the second ring.

"No funny business. You have my word."

Her gaze found his and immediate understanding penetrated through the anger.

She released Uncle Mike and stepped back out of reach. Delaney was smarter than the average woman and a great deal stronger too.

Uncle Mike reached for his throat and winked at John. "I got everything I needed. She clocked you good, kid. You'll probably have a shiner."

Uncle Mike had used his gift in the position she'd held him in. The skin-to-skin contact was all his uncle would need to see Delaney's recent actions play out behind his mind in living color, like a special movie viewing for his pleasure. He'd probably learned more about Delaney in those few minutes than anyone else standing in the room.

Mike moved to the window and pulled out his phone as John went to Delaney. His gaze raked over her, and his hands skimmed her arms, assessing that she hadn't been hurt. She swatted at his hands, her line of sight following Mike's pacing. "What is he doing?"

"I need you to pick up your tail. We have new charges to press."

"What?" Her words came out a whisper as Mike turned to look at John. "Isn't that right, kid? He pulled a gun on a federal officer and threatened a civilian."

"I didn't take the job, Uncle Mike. I don't work for them."

Mike shrugged. "Semantics. He still threatened her and you." His eyes narrowed on Delaney. "You know, you look just like your mother."

Delaney's eyes grew wide but she remained quiet.

"Yeah, I know about your mom. I just got her records when I got your full name."

John turned toward Delaney. "What is he talking about?"

She shook her head.

"Until you know more about your girl there, you better lock up your valuables, kid. Sticky fingers may run in the family."

"Wait...how do you..." Her words trailed off when John grabbed her hand and escorted her to the door.

"Let's go." He nodded at his mom in passing.

John needed to get Delaney out of there before she thought the entire house was against her. He had her at the bottom of the stairs before she yanked him to a stop. "You promised."

"I know, Delaney. I have to grab a bag and we need to get your backpack."

She reluctantly gave in and pulled her hand from his, following him back up into the rooms.

"How did that man know what happened outside the bakery?"

He'd known it was only a matter of time before she asked. John grabbed her backpack from the floor in the closet, where he'd originally placed it, and tossed it on the bed. "That man is my Uncle Mike."

John chewed his lip while trying to think of a suitable lie to tell the smart vixen reporter.

He shook his head against his thoughts. "I don't want any lies between us, Delaney. With that said, it's not my story to tell. We don't know each other well enough for me to tell you the truth. You're just going to have to trust me on this."

He read the indecision on her face. He moved into his room, packed a bag, and tossed the knife inside. When he returned, it was evident she still hadn't made up her mind. "Delaney...will you trust me."

Seconds ticked by while he held his breath. She nodded and grabbed her bag, following behind him as he grabbed her suitcase too. He paused in the foyer in front of his mom and dad and set the suitcase and bag by his feet. He wrapped his arms around his mother's shoulders to ease some of the distress written on her face. "This isn't a good idea."

"Mom, I promised, and I won't let her go alone."

He pulled his mom in for a long, reassuring hug and kissed the top of her head. His dad pulled the keys out of his pocket and handed them to him. "Take my car and, if you need a place to stay, you're welcome to go to the Grove. It has decent security."

His father clasped John's outstretched hand and pulled him in for a manly hug with a pat on the back. 'You still have the watch Uncle Jake gave you?"

John raised his wrist to show the GPS-enabled watch to his father.

"Call us if you need anything. We're working the case on our end and I'll keep you informed too. We're already tracking the Jessups and Uncle Jake has a team on the scumbags already in town. I'm sure Mike will keep them in interrogation for as long as possible."

John nodded. "Thanks, Dad."

John picked up their bags and carried them to the car, stowing them in the trunk while Delaney slid into the passenger side. He slid behind the wheel and released his pent-up breath. "Where to?"

CHAPTER 6

"I haven't thought that far ahead. I guess back to the hotel."

Not likely. John raised his brow and continued out of the security gate. Over his dead body would he hand-deliver Delaney to the Jessup gang, assuming any hadn't been locked up. Now he needed to make her come to the same conclusion that her suggestion was a bad one.

"It's the only hotel in Southall."

He let those words sink in before continuing. She was a smart girl, cool and calculating. She'd realize he was right.

"Come to think of it, I'm sure it's just a misunderstanding and, when Richie gets to town, we can all sit down and discuss this like adults. You can explain that it was all just a big mistake."

He kept a straight face and glanced at her again. Her eyes narrowed, and she crossed her arms.

"Point made, hotshot, but considering it's the only place in town, I guess it will have to do." She shrugged. "Besides, I only have to lay low for forty-eight hours until I meet my informant."

He hadn't been expecting a retort. Delaney's stubbornness was going to get her killed.

"How does a secluded cabin sound? Someplace where you'll be off the grid and out of sight."

"How much security?"

He gave her a lopsided grin and took a right instead of a left heading out of town. "Just me. Maybe we can do some more research on the dagger to pass the time."

Delaney rubbed her lips together, her fingers clutched around her pendant while she contemplated his offer. He needed to seal the deal. He needed to make sure she saw things his way. He reached for her hand and entwined their fingers.

"Consider the benefits." He wiggled his brows.

She rolled her eyes and turned to look out the window.

"Get your mind out of the gutter, woman. I was talking about the dagger and not having to always look over your shoulder." He shrugged. "Besides, I'm an excellent cook, much better than any room service the hotel offers, and it appears we need to get to know each other better."

Delaney slid her fingers from his and turned in her seat. "I don't care about your cooking, Bennett."

"John," he reminded her.

"My personal life is none of your business, John." She took a deep breath. "But you'll give me unrestricted access to the dagger?"

He glanced at her, his gaze caressing her face. Either he was an idiot or a genius. The next seventy-two hours would tell. She wanted the dagger and he wanted her. "Yes."

A sly grin stretched across her lips. "You've got yourself a deal, John. Where's this cabin?"

"On the outskirts of town, away from prying eyes, where no one will bother us."

Delaney cleared her throat. "Listen, I know you're only trying to do me a favor, and I'm grateful, even though I don't show it."

John glanced at her before looking back at the road. "You ready to tell me the whole story?"

"No." Her answer came without hesitation.

John sighed. "Fine."

****

John turned into the dirt driveway that led through the orange grove. The house was off the beaten path and barely visible from the main road, just like he'd said. Her shoulders eased as hope blossomed in her chest that she just might be able to keep out of sight while waiting for her informant, Vinnie, to show. The bastard better have the location she was looking for.

She'd take whatever she could get. The knife and photo were a good start. Her mom had used both as insurance to keep Ritchie at arm's length when she'd fled. Delaney had different plans for their use, assuming she could find the other piece. Plans that would ensure Ritchie Jessup went to jail where he belonged.

John parked the car and grabbed the bags. He slid a panel along the wall, revealing a well hidden security scanner. He pressed his hand against the panel. High tech. Her mom taught her at the ripe age of ten about different security measures. It wasn't until her mom started to settle down that she confessed where she'd learned the information. The scanner ran up and down his palm before the door clicked open, and he walked inside.

"Welcome to the Grove."

She stepped in behind him and turned in place. It was a cabin all right, a log cabin, complete with a large fireplace.

"This place is great."

John disappeared down the hall with the bags, returning moments later with his hands shoved into his pockets. "This is it. The kitchen is there." He gestured toward the kitchen before pointing down the hall. "The bedroom and bath are down that hall, along with a small office where I can access the security monitors hidden around the perimeter.

"You said bedroom, as in single?"

"We'll work that out." He stepped into the kitchen and called back to her. "You thirsty, want a drink?"

She moved in behind him. "You don't have to wait on me, Bennett. I'm a big girl."

Delaney moved to the fridge and opened the freezer. She held in her grin, finding what she was looking for. She reached in and pulled out a bag of frozen peas.

"If you're hungry, I can make something better than peas."

Her grin grew and she shook her head. Stepping closer to him, she cupped his cheek, gently pressing the cold bag against his eye and cheekbone. "It's not for eating, Bennett."

"John."

"I'm sorry I overreacted."

John slid his fingers over hers, holding the bag in place. "We need to work on our communication, Delaney."

Delaney slid her fingers free. "No need for that. I won't be here long enough to worry about it."

"Del—"

Her brows dipped and she instinctively stepped back. "It's better this way. Besides, once this is over, I'm sure another girl will occupy your dreams."

She'd been in town for less than two days, yet she was finding herself fond of the Bennett's, even with their unorthodox way of helping.

Del needed to hurry her mission along and get out fast, before they looked further into her past and found things better left dead and buried.

John tossed the bag of peas into the sink and followed her into the living room, where he started a fire. She kicked off her shoes and curled up on the couch watching John work his magic. "Where do you live?"

"About a mile from the pawn shop."

"Why don't you live here? It's peaceful and quiet."

"Too quiet." John poked at the wood, stirring up red embers. The fire crackled under his ministration. "I grew up here. I went to school here."

"You had your first girlfriend here."

He stood and turned around, placing the poker back into the rack. "I'll grow old and die here, but I've got a lot to accomplish first."

He sat down next to her, ignoring all the other places he could sit. "What about you, Delaney? Where do you live?"

Delaney brought her knees up to her chest and wrapped her arms around them. "I inherited my mom's house when she died, but I have an apartment I prefer."

"I'm sorry about your mom. Don't you have any other family?" She could read the sincerity in his eyes.

Rubbing her lips together, she met his gaze. Dare she tell him the truth? Would he even understand? "My dad wasn't a very nice guy. He was bad news for my mom, taking her down a path that could have killed her. He had bad habits, drugs, stealing, you name it, and he was into them. She was strong, though, a lot stronger than he gave her credit for. She got the hell out of there and took me with her. She started a new life. It wasn't easy. I wasn't an easy kid to raise, but she did the best she could. We both did."

"Del...who's your dad?" John took her hand, stroking small circles on the top.

Shaking her head, she slid her fingers from his grasp. "I told you enough about him."

John's lips slipped into a frown, contention and disappointment on his face. The look was one she was familiar with, but even the empty feeling in her heart wouldn't break down the walls she'd spent decades erecting.

John stood, giving her some much-needed room to breathe. She couldn't think when he was touching her. "Can I get you a drink? Perhaps a glass of wine?"

Suspicion shook her to the core. "Are you trying to get me drunk, Bennett, in hopes I'll share my secrets?"

She tried to pass her question off as a joke, but he wasn't laughing.

He disappeared into the kitchen, returning moments later with a beer in each hand. He handed her one. "It must be tiring being you."

She sipped the beer and tilted her head with the mouth of the bottle still at her lips. "Why do you say that?"

He shrugged before taking a seat on the red bricks of the hearth. "You keep everyone at arm's length, never trusting anyone to share the load or help you. Not all guys have a secret agenda."

"No?" She smirked. "Care to tell me yours, Bennett?"

"Mine is simple really. Help you so I can have my dreams back, get the bad guy and throw his ass in jail, and give the knife to my mom. So you see, Delaney, all I want to do is help you. I truly do, but not at the expense of my family getting hurt."

Propping his elbows on his legs, he let the beer dangle between his legs. "Beyond that, I'd like to explore the chemistry between us, but I won't break what little trust we have or our unique friendship. So you don't have to worry there."

Delaney tipped her head back and laughed. The sound of her own laughter wasn't something she heard very often. "Bennett—"

"John," he countered.

"Let's call this what it is. It's a means to an end for both of us. If you think about it, you want your dreams back and I want the dagger. It's just a bonus that I get to hide out with you while waiting on my informant."

She gestured between them. "This...whatever it is, I wasn't expecting. I'm not one of those girls looking for a boyfriend or husband. I'm not naïve enough to think every man I sleep with is going to be the one. Honestly...I don't think it's in the cards for me and I've come to accept that."

"That's bullshit," John said, rising from his seat. His penetrating gaze landed on her, holding her captive.

Embarrassment shot through her body, heating her cheeks. "That's not bullshit, Bennett. That's reality."

She rose to make her point, planting her hands on her hips. "The majority of us can't live in the fairytale world you have of family and friends or be all goody two shoes, wanting peace, love, and happiness. It's not realistic."

He closed the distance between them in two long, powerful strides. She lifted her chin and cocked her head. She wouldn't back down, not to the likes of him.

"John," he corrected her while cupping her cheek. His presence surrounded her like a warm blanket. He lowered his head, his lips inches from hers. "You're just scared, Delaney. Let me in. Let me help you. Let me show you how great things can be. You just have to let your guard down and I'll do the rest."

"Why you..." She'd balled her fist, ready to knock him on his ass, when John pulled her into his arms and stole her reply with a kiss. All of the anger and self-righteousness fled from her body as she fell farther into his warm embrace. For just a minute, she surrendered and soaked in the feel of everything John.

She leaned into him, clasping her fingers behind his neck. She took charge, parting the seam of his mouth with her tongue and slipping it inside. Caressing, dueling, and tasting what John offered. He wanted her soul, something she couldn't give... but a kiss, surrendering to the heat... Well, that was different.

His large hands were splayed on her back. His muscular body pressed deliciously against her chest. His fingers traveled a path up to her neck, entwining in her hair. Desire pooled in her belly. The need to be closer was overwhelming.

He slowed the kiss, ending the connection much quicker than she'd expected and wanted. His labored breathing matched the rhythm of his heart while he rested his forehead against hers. "Damn."

"John." His name rolled off her tongue, the way she might talk to a lover.

His lips tilted up at the corners and a sign of appreciation appeared on his face. "Yeah?"

"Take me to bed."

His exhaled, releasing a long breath, sliding his eyes shut. "Damn, Del."

"You want this...I want this...what's stopping you?"

****

John released her and stepped back, putting some much-needed distance between them. He did want her. His shaft pressed painfully against his zipper as proof. But as much as he did, he knew it would be nothing more than a one-night stand. As good as it would have been to be inside of her...

"Quit thinking so hard." She stepped over to him, rubbing her hands up his chest. "Sexual pleasure, nothing more... Take what I'm offering."

"Del." He cupped her cheek. "You have no idea how badly I want you. How fucking crazy you make me."

She cupped him through his jeans. "I think I do."

He hissed through gritted teeth.

Delaney ran her hand up his body. "Let me make this easy for you."

She stepped back and tugged her shirt over her head, letting the material slide through her fingers and drop to the floor. She unhooked her bra and all rational thought left him.

Unable to stop himself, he reached for her. Cupping her bottom, he lifted her into his arms. Her long legs wrapped around his waist. She pressed her lips to his as he stumbled, bumping off the walls to get her to a bed. Urgency and need quickened his pace, overshadowing any good intentions or logic.

He eased her down onto the bed and covered her body with his. He made love to her mouth. She moaned deep in her throat, and he knew he needed to slow down and give her the pleasure her body was begging for. He broke the kiss and rolled off to her side. His breathing was heavy, his need overwhelming. He cupped her breast, gently squeezing the mound between his fingers. His mouth latched on to the other one. His tongue swirled around her dusty rose nipple and, when he scraped his teeth against the tender flesh, her nipple pebbled. Her fingers slid into his hair; she was demanding more.

He trailed a slow path down her stomach and popped the button on her jeans, sliding the zipper down. His fingers toyed with her satin panties before delving beneath the soft fabric. She was smooth, bare to the touch, and he hardened in anticipation.

He ran his finger between her slick folds while watching her face. Her heated gaze remained intent. Her breath came out in pants. Every one of his nerve endings was strung tight.

He watched her eyes slide closed when he pressed a finger into her hot, tight sheath. He slid it out and back in.

She moaned. Her heat clenched his finger, tight, warm, and smooth. She wanted him, her desire evident on his fingers. He licked his lips, wishing for a taste while sliding another finger inside. She moaned louder and cupped her breast. His little vixen was wanting and he was ready to give.

Slow, even strokes and her body clenched him tight. He slid his fingers free and brought them up to his mouth, tasting her sweet nectar and wanting more. He slid her jeans and panties off before climbing between her legs, his own body left wanting and covered in clothing. He would pleasure her, give her what she craved.

"I'm going to taste you, Del." He lowered his mouth to her core and blew a hot breath against her damp folds. A soft moan slipped from her lips. He slid his tongue against her teasingly before he pressed his tongue deeper inside. The taste of her exploded on his tongue, her cream sweet to the taste. He lapped her up like a man on the verge of starvation. Tasting, sucking, taking everything she had to give him and wanting more. He moved to her clit, replacing his tongue with his fingers, first one and then two until he had three plunging inside of her.

His tongue circled her nub. Her moans turned deeper, louder. Between pants, "oh yes" and "don't stop" slipped past her lips.

She lifted her pelvis off the mattress, pressing her core into his face. Her fingers tightened in his hair, holding him in place. Her walls clenched his fingers. She was close. So close.

"Come for me," he whispered against her, swirling and pressing down with his tongue. He hurried his strokes, striving to push her over the edge.

She screamed his name when her orgasm hit. Her channel sucked his fingers in, and he continued stroking while lapping up her juices long after the last tremor left her body.

"Oh God." She tried to catch her breath. He placed one more intimate kiss to the tender flesh before kissing his way back up her naked body, stopping briefly when he reached her mouth. He hovered over her and her body clenched in need. He kissed her long and deep, letting her taste herself before he collapsed to her side and pulled her against his chest.

"John..."

"Yeah." At the sound of her voice, his shaft pulsed, seeking relief he knew would come at his own hand.

"We aren't done."

He kissed her forehead. "Yes, we are."

"But you didn't..."

"I got to taste you. That's all I wanted."

"Hardly." She trailed her finger over his shirt-covered chest, making circles before she laid her palm against his heart. She leaned up on her elbow. "I can even the score."

He shook his head. "Not necessary." He slid from the bed. "I'm going to take a shower and then make us something to eat."

She lay back against the mattress, her naked body tempting him to return. He gritted his teeth, biting his lip as he left her and headed into the bathroom for a much-needed shower and release.

CHAPTER 7

Delaney lay deliciously sated as she heard John start the shower. Her mind toyed with the idea of joining him and taking care of him like he'd done for her, but her heart was telling her just the opposite. So she stayed on the bed, debating which would be the right choice. The dagger flashed in her mind, the real reason she was here, the real reason she was with him. Her gaze scanned the room; she was unable to stop the programming her mom had instilled in her. Closet, drawers, his backpack, all suitable hiding places for the dagger. She shook the thoughts from her head.

"Fuck it." She climbed out of the bed, found her clothes, and redressed. "I'm not going to force him."

Her body tingled while she remembered the feel of his lips against her skin, contradicting the hurt building inside. How could she have been so stupid? Delaney stepped out onto the back porch. The cold night air sent a shiver down her spine as it cooled her heated skin. She took a deep breath, releasing a sigh of frustration.

She pulled the phone from her pocket and slid the screen awake. Three new voice mails waited. None from the one person she missed the most, her mom.

She hit play and listened.

The first one was Marco. "The pigs picked me up because of you, you little bitch, but they couldn't hold me. They'll never be able to hold me. I'll always be smarter than those shitheads."

She hit delete and played the second.

She recognized the voice immediately. Vinnie, her informant, only he sounded....scared.

"I'll meet you on Friday at the warehouse. It's too hot to meet there right now. Come alone and make sure you're not followed. The Jessups are in town, and they are out for blood." There was a loud crash in the background, and then the phone cut out. Her heartbeat quickened. Her mind raced as she replayed the message, trying to see if she could figure out the sound. She saved the message and hit play for the third.

"I hear you're running with a new crowd, Delaney." The evil in her dad's voice made the hair on her nape stand at attention. "If you don't want your new friends to end up like your mother, then you'll find the knife and bring it to me."

Delaney's body tensed. A sinking, sick feeling overcame her. She saved the message, clenched the phone in her hands, and closed her eyes. "Just breathe, Delaney. He won't be a threat much longer." Not if her informant came through.

"Who are you talking to?" John's deep voice came from behind her. She slid her phone and shaky hands into her pockets.

"Myself." She turned to find John, hair wet and fully dressed, leaning against the doorframe. He looked refreshed, mouthwatering. "My informant left a message. He wants to meet on Friday instead of tomorrow. Is it cool if we hang out here for a few days longer than I anticipated?"

"Sure, it's fine. Now, let's get you warm and fed." He held out his hand and she slid her fingers into his. "I'm not sure what's stocked in the kitchen, but I'm sure we can find something until I get to the store."

Delaney sat at the table assessing John while he stirred a pot of noodles on the stove. John was a good man, albeit stubborn. She glanced at the window above the sink and then over her shoulder toward the living room, remembering all of the possible exits in the place, how her mother might try and gain entry the way Ritchie had taught them both, stealing under the darkness of night. All of that was behind her, but the mindset still stood. Her mom had taught her well. It was why she was so good at her job and at uncovering the criminals hiding in plain sight. John stirred cheese into the noodles before sitting a bowl in front of her. Her mother and she had spent many a night eating mac and cheese after they'd escaped her father's clutches. She grinned, the old memories warming her heart.

"I'm guessing by your smile that you like mac and cheese."

She took a bite and swallowed. "Love the stuff. But I haven't had it in forever. It used to be my mom's favorite. Not that she could cook much else."

John sat down in the chair next to her. "Tell me about your mom. What was she like?"

Delaney paused mid-bite before sliding the fork out of her mouth. She hadn't been expecting the subject to come up. No one had ever asked before him. No one had cared enough to ask. "She was a good mom. She had it rough growing up, and then I guess you could say my dad was a bad influence, but she managed to get out and take me with her. She was strong like that."

"Kind of like you."

Delaney's brows rose. She'd never thought of herself as strong. Maybe street smart, but not strong. "What makes you say that?"

John sipped his water and folded his arms on the table, his food momentarily forgotten. "You're not afraid to go after what you want or what you believe is right."

Delaney took another bite and let his words sink in. Is that what he thought of her? She frowned. Her real motives soured her appetite. She set her fork down. "You don't know anything about me, John."

He grinned, confusing her more.

"Why are you smiling?"

He shrugged. "I like it when you call me John."

Delaney rolled her eyes and picked her fork back up. She needed to eat if she was going to keep up her strength. Just a few more days, she told herself. A comfortable silence between them grew while they finished their meal.

John washed the dishes and joined her in front of the fire when he had finished. He handed her a beer and sat down next to her before propping his feet up on the coffee table. "So...why crime?"

"Excuse me?" Her gaze shot to his.

"Why criminal journalism? You said your informant was meeting to give you proof of a crime. How did you get into the criminal aspect instead of something less dangerous like....fashion or something?"

She couldn't help but grin. His questions were more proof that he didn't know her at all. If he had, he would have known the answer to that. "I'm good at it. My editor says I have a mind like a criminal. I can see details that others can't."

"Huh…I don't know if that's a bad thing or a good thing. If that's the case, then why not be a cop or join the FBI? Why just report it instead of helping to catch the bad guys?"

No one had bothered to ask before John. She could have been anything growing up had she been brought up under different circumstances, like in John's cozy little world. She took a long swig of her beer. "I guess I'm not good with authority."

John's cell rang and he pulled it out. "I'm sorry, I have to take this."

She waved him on when he stood and walked into the kitchen.

****

He glanced at the caller ID before answering. "Hello."

"Hey, John."

"Hey, Aunt Emma. Everything all right?"

There was a long pause. John could hear his Uncle Jake in the background. "Just tell him already."

"Listen, Lily said Delaney's mom is creeping her out again. She's adamant that Delaney is in trouble."

John glanced back into the living room. His gaze settled on the back of Delaney's head before he leaned back out of the doorway. "Tell her she's fine. We just ate dinner and now we're relaxing in front of the fire. No one is going to get to her out here."

"John, I don't know why but her mom won't leave Lily alone. She's as cryptic as Momma Mae and don't get me started on Momma Mae's opinion of the woman. She's agitated that another ghost has taken up residence. I don't think the two get along very well."

What the hell was he supposed to say to that? "Aunt Emma, see if Lily or you can get any specifics from her. It would help if I knew what we're dealing with."

"She keeps saying danger, danger but that's all we can make out."

"Okay." John rubbed his hand down his face. "That doesn't help but just keep me posted if she says anything else."

"Okay, sweet pea. Just be careful. I'm sure Delaney is a good girl, but I can't help but worry about what she's getting you into."

"Thanks, Aunt Emma. Love you."

"Love you too."

He ended the call and slid the phone back into his pocket. He had every intention of keeping Delaney close. No one was going to get to her out in the Grove and, if they dared try, he'd be ready and waiting. He returned to the living room to find Delaney still sipping her beer.

"Del...can I ask you a question?"

She glanced over her shoulder as he approached and sat down. "Shoot."

"Do you know how to shoot a gun?"

She gave him a half grin. "Sure, I do. Doesn't everybody?"

Tension eased from his shoulders. Knowing she knew how to shoot would make him feel better about keeping her safe. "Do you still have the gun you pulled on me?"

"Of course."

"Do you have a permit to carry a concealed firearm?"

"I do." She reached over and laid her palm on his arm. "I won't need it. I'll be fine. I'm just going to meet with my informant, see if I can talk you out of your dagger, and then go home and write my story. Nothing is going to happen to me."

He laid his hand over hers. "Just the same, I'll feel better knowing you're carrying one while in Southall."

John fired off a text to his mom letting her know they'd arrived. His fingers stilled over the keyboard as he wondered if Delaney would wear his mom's watch with the GPS tracker in it. He glanced up at her and knew instantly that she wouldn't, so he hit Send without even asking. He'd be with her wherever she went. She wouldn't need it, and God-forbid the woman would think he was proposing if he asked her to wear a piece of jewelry. She would have said no on the spot, just out of spite.

John tossed his phone onto the table next to him and they spent the rest of the evening watching a movie. Hours into the flick, he glanced over to find her propped up against the arm of the couch, her eyes shut, and her body relaxed. He clicked the movie off and scooped her up. She leaned into him, never fully opening her eyes.

"Where we going?" she asked with a sleepy voice.

"To bed," he said as he walked down the hall.

"Are you sleeping with me?"

He laid her down, pulled her shoes off, and shifted the covers around her body. He tucked her in and grinned as she snuggled into the pillow. "Yeah, just rest."

He kicked his shoes off, went back into the living room and set the alarm before returning to the room. He slid up in the bed next to her, fully clothed. It was better that way. The more effort it took to get intimate with her, the longer the time he had to come to his senses. He rolled, keeping his back to her, facing the window, his eyes wide open, his mind wandering. Now that he'd found her, would she be starring in his dream tonight, or would his vision change?

Had he thwarted the danger? There was only one way to find out. He closed his eyes, sank into the feather pillow, and waited for sleep to claim him.

Useless dreams came slowly at first, his family, the FBI, his scar. The visions came later, fast and hard.

Delaney and he were running down a wooded path. Fear gripped him and his breathing grew labored. She squeezed his hand and he looked back at her. She trailed behind, gripping her side. Blood stained the ball gown she was wearing, and her mouth was moving, but he couldn't hear what she was trying to say. He slowed and turned toward her at the same time that shots rang out. Her body jolted forward, collapsing into him. Her body went limp and her eyes slid shut. He lowered to his knees, taking her with him. "Delaney," he screamed.

John jolted upright in the bed, blinking wildly. His heart raced, pounding in his chest. His brow and shirt were damp. His legs were tangled in the sheet, holding him still. Her fingers brushed his back, making small circles like you would do to a child who had a nightmare.

"You okay?"

"Yeah," he answered. His voice came out in a rasp as he swallowed around his dry throat.

She slid from the bed and returned with a glass of water. "I hope to hell I wasn't in that dream."

"You weren't," he lied, not having the heart to tell her the truth. It was just a dream he tried to tell himself, just a dream. Not real. She wasn't hurt. She was alive; they both were. Sun was streaming in through the windows. He sipped the water, feeling like a twit for having been woken from a nightmare.

"Liar." She chuckled. "Wanna tell me about it?"

"No." His answer came without hesitation. He shook his head, slid out of the bed, and walked into the bathroom.

****

Delaney watched him retreat behind the safety of the bathroom door. He wouldn't last in there long. Just long enough to try to dissuade her from asking any more questions. She knew he was lying. He'd called her name in his sleep. That was all the verification that she needed.

Delaney glanced around the room, her previous training inevitable regardless if she wasn't going to take the knife. It was engrained in her being. Her eyes landing on every hiding spot that she could think of. He'd said he was bringing it with him. Now she just needed to talk him into giving it to her.

She gave one more glance around the room before she made her way to the kitchen to start a pot of coffee. She was leaning against the counter, waiting on the coffee to brew, when he entered ten minutes behind her - shirtless with wet mussed hair, using a towel to wipe the water from his face. Her heart fluttered while her gaze ran down his body. The pants did little to hide his reaction to her. Why was he denying himself the pleasure she could give him?

"Good morning."

An easy grin slid on his lips. "Good morning." He walked over to her and reached above her head for two coffee cups. "Did you sleep well?"

He set the cups on the counter next to her and cornered her against the counter with an arm on each side.

"Yes." Her answer came out a whisper.

He brushed her hair behind her ear. The slight touch had her leaning into his feel. His gaze bore into hers as if he was trying to see into her soul. He pressed his lips against hers in a light kiss. "I'm glad."

"John, you know I'm only staying until I meet my informant. This thing between us is temporary at best."

He grinned. "You said my name."

She rolled her eyes but was unable to hide her smile. "I'm being serious."

"I know." He stepped back, putting distance between them. His heat was gone as quickly as it arrived. John moistened his lips and his brows dipped, while he poured them both a cup of coffee and then sat down at the table.

"I was thinking that we'll get breakfast at the diner and then hit the grocery store so we'll have something to eat for the next few days. Does that sound okay?"

She nodded while sliding into the chair opposite of his. "That sounds great, but aren't you worried we'll run into the Jessups?"

"I doubt the Jessups will be out grocery shopping, especially this early in the morning, but if you're worried, you can stay here. I don't mind going by myself."

The thought had entered her mind. She mulled over the possibility of hunting for the dagger while he was gone. She'd have time to look, but she was wondering what type of security might be in the house, and there was also the possibility of getting caught. "I'll go with you, if that's okay."

"Great."

She picked up her coffee and started heading for the bedroom. "Do you mind if I take a shower?"

"Nope. Make yourself at home. Towels are in the linen closet and feel free to use whatever else you need."

"Thanks."

She left John sitting at the table and hurried to shower and change. The quicker they left, the faster they could return. Watching the heat and hunger in John's eyes had turned her on. He'd pleasured her last night, but tonight it was her turn to return the favor. She'd make sure of it. By the time she was ready to go, she found John in the living room texting on his phone. He was dressed and ready. He rose and picked up his keys "Ready?"

"Yep."

The drive into town was uneventful. That was a good thing knowing her father's thugs were around. He pulled into a diner on Main and parked. His gaze scanned the area as he rounded to her side of the car and opened the door.

She climbed out and John guided her into the restaurant, his warm palm settled on her lower back. The bell above the door chimed when they walked in, and all gazes turned toward them. She could hear the whispers as they walked by.

She straightened her shoulders and headed for the farthest booth that lined the windowed wall. She slid in and whispered, "Why were they all staring at us?"

He shrugged. "I have no clue."

An old woman with white hair walked over to the table and grinned. "John, it's so nice to see you back in town."

"Thanks, Mrs. A. It's good to be back."

"Well, aren't you going to introduce me to your new friend?"

John made the introductions as Mrs. A pushed on his shoulder for him to slide over. "How are you liking Southall, Delaney?"

"It's lovely."

The old woman nodded. "I see. Well, I ran into John's mom at the coffee shop and she mentioned you might be sticking around for a while."

What was this old woman getting at? Was she truly interested or just a little busybody up in everyone's business? "No, afraid not. Only a few days at the longest."

Mrs. A. gave a slow nod. "What brings you to our little town, business?"

Oh yeah, Delaney had her number. She was fishing.

"Delaney is just passing through. I thought I'd show her around while she's here," John answered.

"Mmm hmm." The woman crossed her arms on the table and tilted her head while she held Delaney's gaze. Would this lady ever leave?

"I don't suppose you know anything about the other visitors in town?"

"Oh?" Delaney's gaze shot to John's, even as she shook her head. "Nope, I'm here alone, but you say there are others from out of town?"

"A couple of them just left. I'm surprised you didn't pass them when you walked in. They're up to no good if you ask me."

John turned his attention to the window, his gaze scanning the area. "You say they just left?"

"Yep. Today it was one guy all by himself, but I could tell he was with the others from yesterday. They all looked the same if you ask me, but this one was different. He was larger and looked mean, not friendly at all."

John gestured for Mrs. A. to move so he could stand. "Excuse us, Mrs. A. We have some errands to run that I forgot about."

"I didn't mean to scare you off, John. I don't suppose the man will be back."

John grinned and held out his hand to Delaney. "Oh, you didn't. I just forgot we have to get going."

Delaney rose and John grabbed her hand, entwining his fingers through hers. "It was good seeing you, Mrs. A."

She nodded. "He's staying at the hotel. I suggest you avoid that area."

Delaney realized in that moment that Mrs. A. knew way more than she was saying. She probably knew everyone's secrets in town.

"It was nice to meet you," Delaney called back as John pulled her out of the restaurant and walked her to the SUV.

She slid inside as she watched the people in the parking lot, trying to get a good look at the people in the surrounding cars. She didn't see her dad anywhere.

John hurried around to the driver's side and got in. "I think we need to go back to the Grove."

She shook her head. "I don't see him. He probably went back to the hotel. I think we're okay to go to the grocery store. It's like you said, he isn't going to be shopping."

"A quick in and out. Something for lunch and dinner and then I'll send my mom or one of my aunts to pick up the rest."

She placed her palm on his arm. "Everything is going to be okay. He won't attack me in a grocery store."

John threw the SUV into reverse and backed out of the spot. "You never know. We're still going to make it quick."

She nodded and clutched her purse closer. She could feel the heavy metal inside, reassuring her that, if the man did happen to appear, she was covered either way.

The grocery store was just up the block, a quick drive. The parking lot was full so John had to park near the back. She could read the worried look on his face. "Maybe we should wait."

"Let's grab a few things, hit the express checkout, and we'll be back in the car in fifteen minutes." Delaney pushed her door open, giving John no other option but to follow.

The store was hopping with people. A quick look in the carts around her explained why. Turkeys, hams, and everything that was synonymous with Christmas dinner festivities overflowed the carts. She sidestepped a cart that was in her path. John grabbed a buggy and began to push. A mother with small children was having a difficult time trying to keep them corralled. Her children would throw something into their cart, and she would grab it and put it back on the shelf. The woman had her hands full.

"Any food allergies, anything specific you want?"

Delaney's stomach chose that moment to growl. "Typical breakfast stuff and maybe something easy for lunch, but how about a steak for dinner? Is there a grill at the Grove?"

John gave her a duh look and grinned. "Of course, and that sounds good."

They made their way around the grocery store, stopping on every aisle. In the back of her mind, she didn't want to think about everything going on. She just wanted to enjoy John's company. He joked with her and they laughed, all the while keeping an eye on their surroundings. He picked up whipped cream and whispered in her ear exactly what he wanted to do with it. He rubbed her arms in the freezer section, the small move warming more than just her arms. Damn, he was sexy. Her heart fluttered from each flirtatious move and touch of his hand. Yes, he was getting his tonight; that was inevitable. She needed to get control, and fast, before she molested him in public. A quick trip to the ladies room to splash some cold water on her face would do the trick.

They rounded the corner of the meat section to pick out steaks. "Where is the restroom?"

John's brows dipped. "On the other side of the store."

He began to push the buggy away without getting their dinner.

"I can go. Just find me a nice, juicy piece of meat."

His lips split into a grin. "I've got a nice piece of meat just waiting for you."

"Oh, I plan to have some of that too," she teased. "I'll be right back."

She glanced over her shoulder as she walked down the aisle. John's hungry gaze was trained on her ass. Delaney could read the desire in his eyes. She was making a mental note to ask him about condoms when she rounded the hallway into the restroom. She took her time, using a wet paper towel against her neck. Images of what John had done to her the previous night were fresh in her mind. "Keep it together, Del."

With her hormones freshly under control, she'd stepped out of the door when a beefy arm snaked around her covering her mouth while a sharp blade was held against her throat. The smell of cigarettes drifted heavy in the air as her assailant dragged her back into the bathroom she'd just walked out of. He flicked the lock on the door and held her flush against his body.

"I hear you've been a pain in the ass, daughter," her father whispered in her ear.

"Mmmmmm," Delaney mumbled around his hands, trying to pry his fingers away. "Mmmmmm."

"I'm going to remove my hand but, if you scream, I'll kill you."

Delaney narrowed her eyes, but she stilled.

"If you even try to escape, I'll kill your new boyfriend too. Are we clear?"

She gave a little nod, feeling the metal press deeper into her skin.

Her dad removed his hand but kept the knife pressed against her neck.

"Where are the dagger and the photo, Del?"

"I don't know."

Her dad swung her body around to face him. He backhanded her. The sting felt like an explosion on her cheek. "Don't fucking lie to me."

He grabbed her by the hair with the knife now pressed against her chest. "You're useless. I should kill you just like I killed her."

Delaney's heartbeat quickened. She'd suspected, but there'd been no proof who had killed her mom. Now she knew without a shadow of a doubt.

"You bastard," Delaney spat.

The knife pressed deeper, cutting through the fabric of her shirt. Delaney stilled, unable to back away.

"I want the dagger and photo the bitch stole from me. If you don't get them, then I'll start with your boyfriend and everyone he loves, and I'll make you watch as I slice his throat and cut out his heart."

Delaney's heart shattered into a million pieces. She knew getting involved with John was a mistake, but she'd never intentionally cause his family or him harm. She had to stop the sadistic asshole before he made good on his threat. "I'll get them. Just don't hurt anyone."

Her father twisted the knife, making the hole in her shirt larger. "That's a good girl. Don't disappoint me."

"I won't." She smirked.

She'd see the asshole dead or behind bars before she ever gave him the dagger. As real as his threats were, she was now more determined than ever to make the bastard pay for killing her mom. He'd tipped his hand, giving her more of a reason to kick his ass.

"Wipe that smile off your face." She saw his closed fist coming but had little time to react. He hit her hard. Slumping to the floor, Delaney's vision blurred, her eyes slid closed, and darkness sucked her under.

****

John pushed the buggy through the checkout and paid the cashier. He kept glancing over his shoulder, thinking Delaney would show up at any second. He walked outside, loaded the groceries into the SUV, and then went back in to search for her.

His heartbeat quickened along with his step as he walked back to the restroom. A woman screamed in the direction he was headed. He ran, sliding to a stop behind the woman who was holding the door open.

He pushed by her and slid down onto his knees next to Delaney. He raised her head and cradled her against his chest. "Del."

Her eyes slid open.

"Call for an ambulance," John barked to the woman behind him.

"No." Delaney shook her head. "Just help me up and take me home."

The woman had her phone in her hand as John scooped Delaney up into his arms, never letting her feet touch the floor.

"Del, you need a doctor."

She rested in his arms. "No, no hospitals, he'll find me again. He just hit me. Please, just get me out of here."

John carried her to the SUV. His blood pressure rose with each step. He was going to find the asshole that did this to her and exact his own form of punishment. A bruise was already forming on her cheek and a trickle of blood escaped from her lip. With every new injury he noticed, John wanted to beat the shit out of the asshole responsible.

"Who did this?" he asked while easing her into the seat of the SUV.

"My dad." Her eyes slid closed as John buckled her in. "Just take me home."

John hurried to the passenger side. "Del."

She didn't answer.

Crap. He dialed the one person he knew would help. "Mom, I need you."

"What happened?"

"She was attacked. She's alive but has bruising to her face along with a cut. She's afraid to go to the hospital."

"Where are you?" He heard the worry in his mother's voice.

"I'm taking her back to the Grove."

"I'm on my way, and I'll call Aunt Elizabeth."

It helped that Uncle Mike's wife was a doctor, given the amount of injuries his family sustained. John glanced at Delaney, his worry growing more with every passing second. He pushed down on the gas pedal. "Hurry, please, Mom."

"John, she's going to be okay."

"I can't lose her."

There was a brief silence over the line. "We'll meet you there, baby."

****

Ritchie reclined in the passenger seat and waited for the fireworks to happen.

"Did she give it to you?" Marco asked as he tapped the steering wheel.

"She didn't have it, but she will."

They sat in silence and watched Delaney's boyfriend load the groceries in the SUV before walking back into the grocery store.

"You should have killed her," Marco said.

Ritchie shook his head. "I didn't ask for your opinion."

Ritchie glanced at Marco.

"I can't kill her until I have the evidence. If that evidence were to surface, they'd be able to pin me with more killings than just the one in the photo. I need that dagger." He gestured to the boyfriend who had Delaney in his arms and was carrying her out of the grocery store. "And she's going to lead me right to it."

Ritchie smacked Marco's arm. "Follow them, but keep your distance."

Marco started the engine and eased out of the parking lot, following three cars behind the SUV. They watched as the SUV pulled down a dirt road into an orange grove on the outskirts of town. The roof of the house was barely visible from the street.

"You want me to go in?"

"No." Ritchie shook his head. "Not yet, keep driving."

CHAPTER 8

"Delaney." A woman's unfamiliar voice called to Delaney. She inhaled a strong odor and turned her head away from the smell. A small, soft palm was on her cheek. "It's time to wake up."

Delaney struggled to open her eyes, blinking awake to stare at the white ceiling. She turned her head toward the brunette standing nearby. A small smile settled on the woman's face. She was holding smelling salts in her hand. "There you are."

Her smile grew.

"Who are you?" Delaney asked her voice raspy and her throat dry.

"I'm Dr. Bennett, but you can call me Elizabeth. I'm John's aunt."

Delaney tried to sit, but Elizabeth eased her back down. "No, just lie still and let me get a look at your injuries. How do you feel?"

"My head hurts."

A cup of water was held to her lips as Elizabeth eased her head up. "Just take a sip."

Delaney did just that, thankful for the cool liquid as it eased her throat. She laid her head back down. "Where's John?"

"If I had to guess, in the living room, driving his mother crazy with worry." Elizabeth sat down on the bed next to Delaney and slapped on some rubber gloves before poking at Del's head. "I'm going to clean your cut and cover it with a bandage. Do you want to tell me what happened?"

"I was hit. The first time was a slap, but the next he clocked me with his fist."

Elizabeth nodded. "He must have been wearing a ring. It explains the cut." She cleaned the area before applying a bandage. "Did you recognize who hit you?"

Delaney turned her head away from the woman and tried to sit up, but Elizabeth stopped her. "I need to talk to John."

"I'll get him. Just rest, but don't go to sleep. We don't know if you have a concussion, yet."

Delaney nodded and the small movement made her vision blur.

Elizabeth left the room and Del could hear the voices outside. Seconds later, John walked in with a worried look on his face. He sat down next to her and laid a palm on her cheek. "How do you feel?"

"A little dizzy but I'll survive."

"How come you didn't tell me that Ritchie Jessup is your dad?"

She slid her eyes closed. She'd told John that her father had hit her, but didn't tell him it had been Ritchie.

She opened her eyes. "How do you know Ritchie's my father?"

John tilted his head. "There's video surveillance at the store that covers the hallway. You said your dad did this to you, and we recognized Jessup's face as the man waiting for you to walk out."

"Well, we can't all pick our relatives. I told you my dad was a bad guy. My mom left him when I was little."

"He didn't go after her?"

Delaney swallowed around the lump in her throat. If she was ever going to come clean with Bennett, now would be the time. The more he knew, the more danger he was in, but she didn't trust her dad not to follow through regardless. John had a right to know what he'd walked into so he could stay safe, just like she'd had a right to know while growing up.

"My mom took some incriminating evidence and threatened that, if he ever came around either of us, she'd use it. I guess he believed her."

"What evidence?"

"The dagger and a photo."

John's head drooped forward. "So that's where it went when it fell off the radar." He looked up at her. "Why didn't you just tell me?"

"I didn't want to get you involved. When he had me in the bathroom, he threatened you and me. You have the dagger and I still need to find the photo. He wants both, or he's going to kill us."

John rested against the headboard, crossing his ankles. "What I don't get, is if your mom had the dagger, how did it end up in the pawn shop?"

Delaney shrugged. "I don't know. She told me years ago that she separated them so, that even if he found one, he wouldn't find the other. She'd given me a name once and, when I learned he died and his estate was auctioned off, all I had to do was follow the trail."

He nodded and remained quiet for a minute that seemed like an eternity. "Okay, let's not worry about how it got there. Where's the photo?"

Delaney reached for her locket and squeezed. "I don't know, but Vinnie does. At least he says he does."

"Your informant? How do you know he's telling you the truth?"

She nodded. "I never told him about the picture. He's the one that brought it up so, yeah, Vinnie knows and, if I had to guess, he knows more than what he's told me. I'll be sure to find out what else he's keeping from me when we meet on Friday."

"So what was your plan? You'd get the dagger and the photo and what? Expose him in a story?"

"No." Her voice came out a whisper. "I was going to turn them over to the FBI so they could arrest him."

She couldn't help the tear that slid down her face. John lay down next to her and brushed it away with his thumb.

"Is that why you're crying? It must be hard, throwing your dad in jail."

A bubble of laughter slipped out. "He can rot in hell." She rolled to face him. "He told me in the bathroom that he killed my mom. The tear was for her."

"Oh, baby, I'm so sorry." John cupped her cheek before he pressed his lips against hers. He broke the kiss and leaned back. "Don't worry, Del. I'm not going to let anything happen to you."

She wasn't worried about herself. She was worried about him.

"Just relax. I'm going to get you some breakfast and talk to the others."

"Others?" Her eyes widened. "What others?"

John slid off the bed. "Mike and my parents. I have to tell them."

She understood. They needed to know. They were going to hate her, but they had a right to know.

"Okay."

****

John eased the door closed behind him and walked back into the living room to find his parents, Uncle Mike, and Aunt Elizabeth waiting for him.

Elizabeth stood. "I need to finish examining her."

John nodded and waited for Elizabeth to leave the room. They adjourned to the kitchen, poured coffee, and sat down at the table, where John proceeded to tell Mike and his parents everything that Delaney had told him. He'd had to spoil his mom's Christmas present, the whole reason for purchasing the dagger in the first place, but she reminded him it was the thought that counted and it was more important to get a killer off the streets.

"Where's the dagger?" Mike asked.

John tilted his head. "I brought it with me. It's in my black bag by the couch."

"I'm going to need her statement on what happened and what she knows."

John nodded. "I'll bring her in when she feels better."

John's dad placed his hand on his mom's shoulder. "You know, when I touch the dagger with my gift, it's possible that it will take me to the time of the killing."

"I know," John replied while looking down at his coffee cup.

"Have you told her about our abilities?"

His head shot up. "No. She's a reporter. I didn't trust her until now."

"John." His mother's voice was soft. "Why don't you take her to the beach house and let us handle this for you?"

He shook his head. "She wouldn't go. Besides, she's the only one who can figure out where the photo is. You can't put the dagger at the scene of the crime with forensic evidence. We're going to need more proof to place her father at the scene. We need that evidence if we're going to put this asshole away for good."

Abby rose from her seat and rounded the table. She placed her arms around her son, hugging him from behind. She kissed his temple. "Please be careful."

"We will."

John's dad nodded. "We'll see what we can dig up on her mom. Any other property she owned, who her friends were. We'll research it from that end while Delaney and you try to figure this out."

"Thanks, Dad."

Uncle Mike rose. "Be careful, kid, and don't forget to bring her in. We're taking the dagger with us."

John stood and walked to the fridge. "I'm going to fix her something to eat, and we're going to lay low until she meets with her informant."

"That's just what the doctor ordered," Elizabeth said as she walked into the room. "I don't think she has a concussion but, just to be on the safe side, keep an eye on her tonight and try to keep her up as long as possible."

Mike walked over to his wife and tossed his arm over her shoulder. "Thanks, baby."

She smiled up at him, the love in her eyes evident to everyone watching. John wanted a relationship like that one day. All of his aunts and uncles were the epitome of happy. It hadn't always been like that, but it was now.

John ushered everyone out, set the alarm, and fixed Delaney a late breakfast, complete with French toast, eggs, bacon, and orange juice. They spent the rest of the afternoon relaxing and just enjoying each other's company. Day turned into night without another incident.

****

Delaney tried her best to reassure John that she was fine. He doted on her as if she was made of glass and ready to break, but she had an idea of how to break him from the habit. They lay snuggled on the couch, the television a slow mumble in the background. She glanced up at him. "I need a shower." She rose, facing him, and lifted her shirt over her head and dropped it to the floor. She took a few steps back and unhooked her bra, still keeping eye contact with him. She let her bra slide down her arms and dropped that too. "Would you mind helping me wash my back?"

"Del..."

She ran her hands over her stomach and up to her breasts and gave a little squeeze.

"Please."

"It's not a good idea." The hunger in his eyes contradicted his words.

"What if I fall?" She stuck her bottom lip out, reached for her jeans and popped the button, slowly sliding the zipper down.

John stood up and grinned. "We can't have that."

She smiled and turned around, leaving him to follow her into the bathroom. She was bent over turning on the water when she felt his palms on her hips and his groin pressing against her backside. He leaned over her, his hands cupping her breasts as he brought her back up to a standing position. He massaged the plump flesh, and her eyes slid closed. She shimmied her jeans and panties off and kicked them to the side.

Her hands covered his, lifting one of his palms to her mouth. She sucked his finger inside and felt him harden even more. "Join me."

She grinned as she stepped into the shower, beneath the spray of warm water. Not even a minute later he stepped in with her. His hands and mouth were everywhere, making every part of her tingle. His mouth pressed against hers as his fingers trailed a path down her belly and into her folds. He kissed her through the needy moan that bubbled in her throat.

"You like that, baby?"

"Mmm hmm." She smiled against his lips and reached for him, wrapping her fingers around his long, thick shaft. "Not as much as I'm going to like this."

She stroked him until he was firm and hard, up and down, enjoying the feel of him in her hand. She cupped his balls with the other.

"Damn, Del, you don't play fair."

He slid two fingers inside of her, pumping in and out. "Two can play that game." He increased the speed. Every fiber of her body was strung tight, her orgasm just out of reach.

"I need you in me."

The pressure of his fingers disappeared, and his palms clamped onto her ass as he lifted her off her feet. Wrapping her legs around his waist, he pegged her against the wall while sliding the tip of his cock through her wet folds. He slid in an inch at a time until he was fully seated. He was long and thick, fully filling before he eased back out. His hand landed on her breast as his mouth sought hers out. He plundered her mouth, tasting every crevice, taking what he wanted. His strokes increased in pace. She felt him swelling, his cock throbbing against her folds as she tightened around him, her orgasm close.

He pressed his head into the crook of her neck, holding her in place while he plundered her body, in and out. The sensation started in her toes and coursed through her body, tightening with every stroke, building into a wave of unadulterated lust and desire.

"Come for me, Del," he whispered into her ear.

Her head pressed against the cold tile as her channel tightened, squeezing and milking his cock. She screamed his name as her release overcame her. Her breathing became more labored as he slid in two more times, holding himself fully seated when she felt the warmth of his seed coat her channel.

Their breathing slowed as he pulled out and let her slide down his body.

"We need to do more of that." His voice was hoarse.

"Absolutely." She smiled as he leaned into her.

His kiss was tender and sweet, as was his touch.

They washed each other, dried off, and then lay down in the bed. She was nestled into his side, her arm over his chest. She felt the beat of his heart beneath her palm. "John?" She glanced up at him. His eyes were closed.

"Yeah?"

"What are we going to do if we can't find the photo?"

"We'll deal with that bridge when we get to it." He leaned up and kissed her head. "Get some rest. We have a busy day tomorrow."

CHAPTER 9

They woke early the next morning. Neither of them slept well, even though exhausted from making love. It didn't help that her naked body was pressed into his side. They'd had sex three more times and, by two o'clock in the morning, they'd both fallen asleep from pure exhaustion.

After getting dressed, they ate and sat around for most of the day, even though they were unable to relax. Today was the day they would meet her informant. Today was D-day. She'd only pushed her food around on her plate while constantly checking her phone.

"Relax, Delaney." He stroked her shoulder while she snuggled into his side.

"If he doesn't come through, I'll kill him," Delaney blurted out while clutching her locket.

John pressed his lips to the top of her head. "If he doesn't come through, then we'll figure it out and find it on our own."

He reached down and lifted the locket for a better look. "You know, when you're nervous you have a habit of holding this."

She slid it out of his fingers and raised it so she could see. "My mom gave it to me on my sixteenth birthday. I never take it off."

The shape of the locket was unique. It wasn't a heart like most he'd seen or a rectangle either. It had arms sticking out of the sides with a circle in the middle. It looked more like a bloated cross than anything else.

"Do you have a picture inside?"

She flicked it open, and there was a photo of a woman who looked like an older version of Delaney and Delaney as a small child.

"You were a cute kid," John teased.

"Thanks."

He stroked his fingers down her arm. "We need to get ready." He looked out the back window. "The sun is starting to set and it looks like it's going to rain."

She leaned up and straddled his lap, pressing her lips to his. "Thank you for helping me, John. I don't know what I'd do without you."

John stroked his fingers through her hair. "I'll always help you, Delaney. I know you don't have your mother around anymore, but you have me."

She kissed him one more time before climbing off his lap and going into the bedroom. She was growing on him. She needed him as much as he needed her, and that thought made him pause. Would he ever get his dreams back? His life?

****

Thunder clapped as another streak of lightning lit the gray sky. John had a bad feeling about the meeting. He pulled his trench coat closed and grabbed her hand, leading the way farther into the darkened alley. The iridescent light from the flashlight bounced off the old brick walls as Delaney took each step.

"What do you know about this guy?"

"He promised me proof and I'm sure he'll follow through."

John pulled the gun stashed in his shoulder holster and tightened his grip while stepping farther into the darkened alley which was flanked on both sides by tall concrete buildings. His gut instinct had been to make her wait in the car. His stomach rolled with apprehension. His muscles tightened as he opened the alley door to the warehouse. They were in the old part of town. Abandoned buildings lined the streets and homeless people hung out in the alleyways. The smell of urine and mold hit his nose, almost making him gag, as he stepped into the building. Delaney followed behind him. His hand shot out, stopping her mid-step as he gestured to the ground. Mice scurried over the broken glass in a hurry to hide from the intruders. He moved farther into the building, the fine hair on his arms standing on end.

Delaney stepped up beside him. "Do you smell that?"

"Urine or mold?"

She shook her head, her expression worried. "No...I've smelled this before at my mother's house..." She turned around in place, scanning their surroundings. "The day I found her murdered."

John pulled in a deep breath and tried to separate the smells. The sick coppery scent was mixed with the others. The faint smell of blood made him tense.

"Blood."

Delaney visibly shivered as she stepped deeper into the building and farther down the empty hall. She stopped and drew in a deep breath. "It's stronger over here." She pointed farther up the dank hallway. "It's coming from this way."

John stepped past her, the butt of the gun held firmly in both hands. He followed the smell farther into the building, stopping in front of an unmarked door.

He pressed her against the wall and motioned for her to stay before he pushed the door open with his gun held out in front of him. He stepped into the room; the darkness provided him with as much cover as it did whatever else was in there with him. His boot hit against something lumpy and heavy on the floor, his head telling him what his eyes had yet to see. A body lay on the floor.

The flashlight Delaney had been holding illuminated the room as she stepped over the threshold.

"John," she whispered into the small room before gasping when her light hit the dead guy on the floor. He was lying in a pool of dried blood, his dead body probably several days old.

"No." Her hand covered her mouth and a tear trickled down her cheek as she reached for the unmoving body.

John caught her before she touched him. "Don't touch, Del. They're going to dust for fingerprints."

Delaney's brows creased as she frowned, unable to look away. Her informant's dead body lay sprawled out on the cold concrete floor. "Vinnie."

John glanced down at the man's body which had a knife protruding from his chest. "Please tell me this isn't your informant."

She remained silent as they both bent down to examine her snitch. John took the flashlight from her hands and shined the light on the knife. His eyes bulged when he discovered he was looking at a replica of the Wellborn era knife. How was that even possible and what the hell was going on? "Delaney."

She gasped and pushed to her feet. "Shit."

"Delaney." He pulled his phone from his pocket and speed dialed the number he needed. "You want to explain why a replica of my mom's knife is sticking out of your informant's body?"

He turned when she didn't answer.

She swallowed hard. "It was a present."

John's brows dipped in confusion as he held up his index finger. "Mom, you need to bring your forensic team and Uncle Mike to the abandoned building at Sixth and Jinks. There's a dead body."

He gave her what information he had before hanging up. "It can't be the real dagger; I have that at the cabin."

"Ritchie had another one made, just like the real one, and presented it to my mother on their wedding day." Her words came out a whisper in the quiet room. "Mine was the copy, and yours is the real one. She didn't know which one he'd used to kill, so she took them both."

John glanced back down at the body. "How and why is yours here? This doesn't make any sense." John rubbed his hand over his neck. Nothing made sense. Delaney's informant was dead with a knife she supposedly owned, not to mention that she'd kept its existence a secret all of this time. What did he really know about Delaney Chance?

"I can explain."

His brow rose.

She pointed down to the body. "Not about the murder, but about the dagger. I was going to turn them both in. It was locked up in my apartment. I don't know how it ended up here."

"Why didn't you tell me there were two?" He glanced down at the body before looking back up at her. "Shit. I bet your prints are still on it."

She folded her hands together in front of her. Sirens screamed outside the building, the sound becoming louder the closer the authorities came.

"You better start talking, Delaney. I'm the only friend you've got."

Delaney pursed her lips together and slowly shook her head.

"You know I didn't do this." She pointed to Vinnie while walking around the dank room. Broken furniture lay scattered on the ground, the window slightly ajar. "I've been with you this entire time. He was supposed to have proof. What did he do with my photo?"

John watched Delaney turn from defiant to almost frantic as she moved throughout the room. "Don't touch anything, Delaney. This is a crime scene. The murder weapon is yours. Do you really want to leave prints pointing to yourself as the killer?"

She spun around. "I didn't do this."

"I know you didn't, but you might have a hard time convincing the cops. Let's just hope there are more fingerprints on the dagger than yours."

A look of dismay overtook her face. Her shoulders sagged when the realization, of what he was trying to get through her thick skull, sunk in. He knew this was a setup and he knew she was incapable of murder. His gut told him that she was innocent, even though the evidence pointed to the contrary.

"Why didn't you tell me there were two?"

She lowered her gaze. "It didn't matter. You had the real one."

John heard the shouts and the sounds of boots coming down the hall. He slid his gun back into the shoulder holster and held up his hands, raising a brow until she did too. He wasn't a cop, even though he'd called them in. If anyone other than his family showed up first, he'd look like a suspect. Along with the tight-lipped Delaney Chance.

He turned toward the door. Relief filled his body when he saw that his Uncle Mike was the first to appear. Behind him were his mother and her team of forensic investigators, along with the coroner and few others that John didn't know.

Mike lowered his weapon and holstered it as he pulled John and Delaney off to the side and out of the way as the teams began their work. His mom was already shouting orders for no one to disturb the body until she got a closer look. She walked over to them as Mike began asking questions. John filled them both in on what they were doing there. Uncle Mike was in full business mode, scanning for any telltale sign that either John or Delaney weren't being on the up and up.

"What aren't you telling me?" He glanced back and forth between them. "Spill it."

"Mike," his mom said.

Uncle Mike held up his palm. "Either you tell me now, or I'll take you both down to the station and you can tell me there. Which is it going to be?"

"The dagger is mine. But I didn't kill him."

"How do you know the deceased?" Mike pegged her with his demanding glare.

"He was her informant," John answered.

"I didn't ask you, kid. I asked her." Mike glanced at John. "Does she have an alibi?"

John glanced past his uncle's shoulder to the body on the floor. "She's been with me since the day she arrived in town."

"John." He heard the disapproval in his mother's voice. "Tell him everything."

"In my dream, she was talking to this guy in the alleyway. I saved her that day when the Jessups showed up and I hauled her ass out of there. Then she disappeared until the next morning."

"Where did you go? Who can corroborate your whereabouts?"

She lowered her head. "I went to the coffee shop when I left John."

Mike threw his hands up. "So you mean to tell me that's the best you've got?"

John's gaze flew to Delaney's guilt-stricken face.

She looked up. "I didn't do this." Her eyes lit up. "He left a message on my phone, and there was the sound of a crash in the background." She reached for her empty pocket and turned to John. "My phone is at the Grove."

Mike gestured to the door. "Delaney Chance, I'll need to take you in for questioning. John, you can meet us at the station."

Abby placed her palm on John's arm, stopping him from leaving. "John, you know I'll be able to get a read on the dagger. We'll know what happened as soon as we get him processed, but in the meantime, you need to get her phone."

"Mom," John said through gritted teeth.

"Honey." She turned him to look at her instead of the doorway Mike and Delaney had just left through. She cupped his arms. "The next few hours will either make or break whatever relationship or trust you two share. Think twice before you accuse her of anything. We both know there are always extenuating circumstances."

She was talking about his dad. They'd both accused him of being less than honest about his intentions when he'd shown back up in their lives. And they had both been wrong.

"She didn't tell me there were two." He pulled his arm from her grasp and stomped out the door toward the exit. Delaney Chance had a lot of explaining to do, not only to the authorities but to him as well. It was high time he learned the truth, and he was not in the right frame of mind to listen to her lies.

He slid behind the wheel of his dad's car. Delaney's purse lay in the passenger seat. A purse she normally had on her at all times. He picked it up and slid it open. Her phone lay on top of the gun she carried. He switched it on to find that it was password protected. If she was telling them the truth, then it would be in her voicemails, time stamped and tied with a nice little bow.

****

John pushed through the doors at the precinct and checked in at the desk. They all knew John was Abby's kid and waved him through. His heart pounded the closer he got to the interrogation rooms. He glanced at one of the detectives. "Uncle Mike in there?"

He nodded. "He's interrogating someone. You want to wait in his office?"

John shook his head and opened the door. Delaney was seated at the table and had tear streaks down her face. Mike was standing on the other side of the table with his arms crossed over his chest. John handed her the phone. "It's password protected. Play him the message."

She typed in her password, put it on speaker, and started the message.

"Saved messages. Wednesday four p.m.," an automated voice said before it switched to the message.

A voice filled the room, the same voice of the man John had heard her talking to in the alley the first time he'd laid eyes on her. "I'll meet you on Friday at the warehouse. It's too hot to meet there right now. Come alone and make sure you're not followed. The Jessups are in town, and they are out for blood." There was a loud crash in the background, and then the phone cut out.

"She's been with me since this message, when he was alive. She didn't have the opportunity to kill him and, even if she did, she wouldn't have because he was the only person who knew the location of the evidence she needs to help convict her father."

John held out his hand to Delaney. "Let's go."

She glanced between John and his uncle, confusion spread across her face. "Can I?"

Mike held out his hand. "The phone stays. We'll need to save that message for evidence. I'll get it back to you as soon as we're done. Since John is vouching for the remainder of your time, you're free to go."

John nodded. "I will and I am."

Mike held out his hand and waited for Delany to take it to shake. He held it mere minutes before he let go. John knew his Uncle had just used his gift to see if they were telling the truth. Even if she didn't.

John steered Delaney out of the offices and to the waiting SUV; he opened her door, waiting for her to slide in before he got in the other side. "You didn't believe me until you heard the message, did you?"

John took a deep breath and started the SUV. "Of course I did."

"No, you didn't."

He drove back to the Grove. The silence between them was thick and uncomfortable.

When he pulled in he turned the car off. She tried to get out, but he stopped her.

"Delaney." He turned in his seat. "I believed you because I knew there was no way I could be falling for a woman who was capable of that."

"John..."

He shook his head. "I know. You told me this is just temporary." He shrugged. "I can't help what I feel."

With that said, he didn't wait for her reply. He got out of the SUV and headed for the door. He could feel her behind him. Unsaid words hung in the air.

The door was ajar, and the lights were off, and John knew he hadn't left things like that. He slid his gun out of his leg holster and held his finger to his lips while gesturing toward the break-in.

She nodded.

John silently stepped into his father's house and tightened his grip on the gun. His eyes scanned the area and his heart raced. His father was going to kill him if the intruders didn't do it first. The room was in shambles. The cushions were off the couch and sliced open, the stuffing scattered around the room. The coffee table was overturned; one of the legs broken and splintered. Paintings hung crookedly on the walls. Broken picture frames lay near his feet with the glass shattered. Stuff was scattered and broken everywhere.

Delaney stepped up behind him. Her breath hitched, the small noise came from behind him. "Oh my God."

He held up his hand, stopping her from entering any farther and leaned closer to whisper in her ear. "I need to make sure they aren't still here. Don't move."

She nodded as he went to see what other damage had been done.

The rest of the house was worse. The bed comforter was sliced and discarded. Everything from the closet lay on the floor in the room. Dresser drawers were pulled out and overturned. There was a smell he couldn't pinpoint. Something that didn't belong. The mattress had been shoved and overturned from the bed. The stuff from Delaney's backpack was pulled out.

The door to his father's office was left ajar. John inched it open the rest of the way with the barrel of his gun. The security monitors were smashed on the floor. A knife was stuck into the hard drive of the computer. The drawers from the desk were on the ground.

John moved to the safe on the wall, the door hanging open from just one hinge. Whatever contents had been in there were gone. Black charred marks were burned on the steel near the combination. His heart squeezed in his chest. Whoever had done this was going to pay.

"John," Delaney called.

John scanned the room one last time, hoping that maybe his mom would be able to get some prints that might have been left behind.

"John," Delaney yelled with more urgency.

Stepping out of the room, John returned to the living room to find her right where he'd left her.

"Yeah?"

She took a deep breath. "You smell that?"

He inhaled and his eyes widened. "Gas."

She nodded in agreement.

His gaze flew to the kitchen. The knobs on the stoves were in the on position but the little blue flame beneath the burner was missing. He didn't have time to look for the trigger that would start the chain reaction that was going to kill them. His gut clenched.

"Shit." He hurried toward her and grabbed her hand in a tight grip. "Run," he screamed, panic in his voice. He ran for the door, making sure she was at his side. He didn't stop at the SUV; they didn't have time. They'd run through the orange grove, past several trees, when the unthinkable happened.

He glanced back as the windows blew and shards of glass exploded. Heat licked his back as the force of a blast knocked them to the ground. He inched to cover her with his body as debris and wood shot through the air. He covered his head as remnants from the broken furniture landed nearby.

"Stay down," he demanded, glancing back toward the house. The stove from the kitchen was imbedded into the hood of his father's SUV. Red and orange flames danced in the moonlit sky. Black smoke and soot made it hard to breathe. Flames were consuming the house. He rolled off Delaney and helped her to sit up. John holstered his gun, but his heart raced as adrenaline coursed through his body.

"Are you hurt?" John asked while palming Delaney's face.

"No."

John ran his hands down her arms over her goose bumps, assessing everything before he turned back to watch what was left of his dad's house burn.

"My dad's going to kill me," John said in a state of shock.

"I think mine just tried," Delaney uttered.

He pushed off the ground and held out his hand to help her. He pulled her up into his arms and against his chest. She trembled as he held her close. The fear of almost losing her outweighed everything that was lost.

He felt the vibration of his phone in his pocket and knew it was his family. His Aunt

Emma had probably put everyone in a panic state that someone was in trouble. He dug into his pocket and pulled out his phone. He'd just pressed the answer button when he heard the siren's getting closer.

"Are you all right?"

"We are, but your house isn't."

The line went momentarily silent before his mother spoke again. "Aunt Emma called. We're already on our way."

"Thanks, Mom."

The ambulance and fire trucks arrived at the same time. He'd insisted they check Delaney to make sure she wasn't hurt. John crossed his arms over his chest while they watched the firemen douse the flames.

His parents' SUV screeched to a halt. His mother flew out of the passenger side and into John's arms. She squeezed him tight before leaning back, her gaze assessing. "Are you hurt?"

"No. We're both fine."

She nodded. "I'm going to kill this bastard."

"Not if I find him first," his father said as he approached. Abby left them and headed to where Delaney was being checked by the paramedics. "What happened?"

"The place was ransacked when we got here. Everything in your safe is gone."

"You went in?" his father asked. Concern strained his voice.

John nodded. "We didn't smell the gas until it was almost too late."

He tossed his arm around his son's shoulders. "Thank God you're all right."

"I'm sorry, Dad."

"What were they after?"

John glanced back at his mother talking in hushed tones to Delaney.

"My money is on Ritchie Jessup and I'm betting he was after the Wellborn dagger I bought Mom for Christmas."

His father dropped his hold and crossed his arms over his chest. He stroked the fine hairs on his chin. "The one you turned over to Mike?"

"Yeah. I just don't know how he got through your security."

"Time will tell. I'll review the uplink to the cameras in the Grove and see if we got a clean picture of the parties responsible and how they managed to get in." His dad paused before turning to look at John. "I think it might be best if you let your mom and me handle this from here on out."

John let out a lengthy sigh, his gaze landing on Delaney. She was looking at him. Her shoulders were slumped, her eyes tired. She was exhausted; they both were. "Wish we could, but Delaney's the only one who can find the photo."

"What if we get Aunt Emma to try and talk to her mom again? Maybe they can get the location from her."

He patted his dad on his shoulder. "Any help we can get would be great. You do that, and we'll keep searching." He nodded toward the ambulance. "I'm going to take her back to my house. She looks like she's about to fall over from exhaustion."

They both walked over to the ambulance and John held out his hand. She entwined her fingers through his. "I'm taking her back to my place." John glanced over his shoulder to the fire crews and police on the property. "Can you take care of this?"

"Of course we can," Abby piped in. Her brows dipped when she held his father's gaze. He could read the worry on her face "You go rest."

John glanced over to the ruined SUV and his shoulders sank.

His father pulled out his keys and handed them over. "We'll catch a ride back with the guys from the police department."

"Thanks, Dad." John led Delaney over to his father's SUV and opened her door. They drove back to his place in silence. Delaney sat in the passenger seat, looking lost in thought. Her head was propped against the window as she worried her bottom lip between her teeth.

There was no telling what she was thinking; her face was unreadable.

CHAPTER 10

Delaney stared out the window, no longer focusing on the passing scenery. She had no clue where he was taking her and, honestly, she didn't care. It was her fault they were in this mess. Her fault that he'd almost died. She couldn't let it happen again. She just couldn't.

"Don't even think about it." John's voice broke through her fog, pulling her out of calculating the next move. The next move without him.

"Don't think about what?" she asked, straightening in her seat.

"It's not your fault." He glanced over to her. "Do you hear me? This is not your fault."

Regardless of whether or not he wanted to admit it, it was her fault. It was her father, and it was her past that had almost stolen John's life.

"How do you know what I'm thinking? Can you read minds now too?"

"I don't have to be able to read your mind. Your silence tells me enough." John reached for her, entwining their fingers. "We'll get through this."

"John..."

"No, Del. We're going to find the photo and take this bastard down together." He glanced at her. "We're going to do this together."

John had a good heart. He was the kind of man who, in any other circumstance, she might try to have a relationship with.

He pulled up in front of a one-story house in the middle of a suburban neighborhood. "Come on, you're exhausted."

She nodded, releasing his hand. What she needed was a good night's sleep. One full night, then she'd come up with a plan in the morning to get him to forget about her.

John led Delaney into the house with his palm on her lower back; she paused just inside the door as he locked it behind them and set the alarm. The alarm wouldn't keep Ritchie out. She knew it and he knew it. It was a false sense of security but, regardless, it was the one place that they hadn't been yet. Since Jessup knew about the Grove, there was a good chance he knew about Aunt Claire's house. There was no way in hell he was taking her back there tonight. Not yet, not until they made a plan.

John pulled her into his arms and pressed his lips to hers in a kiss that was meant to comfort but did anything but. His mouth plundered as he trailed a path with his fingers up and down her back. Their tongues dueled as she took her time enjoying and savoring his taste, wanting the memory of this moment for the dark nights ahead.

When he broke the kiss, he leaned his forehead to hers, each of them breathing hard. "Del, I need you."

She reached for the hem of her shirt and pulled it over her head, letting the material slide free from her fingers. "Take me."

And that was exactly what he did. He lifted her into his arms and carried her down a long hall and into the bedroom. His mouth latched on to hers, and he eased her down onto the bed. He'd savored her; he'd kissed her; he'd owned her the rest of the night in a way no man before ever could. His needs matched her own. This night would forever be etched into her mind, a night and a man who she'd compare against all others.

Night turned into day as they lay in the bed, their sweat-slicked bodies cooling as they caught their breaths. He tugged her closer, nestling their bodies together as she rested her head in the crook of his arm. Her hand lay against his chest, the rhythm of his heart reminding her that they were both still alive. She let exhaustion consume her, stealing away her worries.

****

Ritchie leaned against the trunk of a large oak tree in the forest beyond the Grove. The chill in the night air touched his cheeks. He slid out of sight as fire trucks and ambulances passed by to fight the flames that were shooting high. He was a bastard for trying to kill his own kid. Yet that was the least of his concerns.

"You don't have the photo yet. Why did you try to kill her?" Marco asked from next to him as he watched the scene play out.

"Motivation," Ritchie said, tilting his head. He watched as his daughter climbed into another SUV before he gave the signal to Phil, his third-in-command that was waiting in a nearby car, for him to follow. He'd brought his third-in-command on a whim, and it had been a wise move. He'd already ordered them to stay close should she leave, but not close enough to be caught. Where his daughter went, he'd go, until he had the fucking photo in his hand. And, if there were duplicates that miraculously surfaced, those people would suffer the same fate. They'd be dead just like all the rest of the people that tried snitching on him in the past.

"How did you know she'd get out in time?"

Ritchie's lip twitched. "She's my daughter. It's going to take a hell of a lot more to kill her than that. It's in her DNA."

"Yeah, but you couldn't have known for sure."

Ritchie's blood pressure was rising. He pulled his gun and pressed the barrel to the head of his second-in-command, Marco. "Are you questioning me, you stupid punk?"

Marco held up his hands. "No, man. I'd never do that."

Ritchie lowered his gun, striking Marco with the back of his hand. Marco dropped to his knees, and Ritchie hit him again, one more time, for being stupid. "I run this show. You don't question me." Ritchie squatted next to Marco. "Now get your ass in the car."

Ritchie slid into the passenger seat and tapped his finger on his leg while Marco drove. Delaney's time was coming, but it wasn't today.

"Did you at least figure out where Vinnie was staying before you killed him? That son of a bitch had to have stashed my picture somewhere."

Marco shook his head. "Not yet. I've got a couple of our guys shaking down his acquaintances. We should know by tomorrow."

"Good. About time you did something right." Ritchie sneered. His daughter was smarter than he gave her credit for. She was a mixture of both her mom and him, cunning and smart. He'd have been proud to take her under his wing and teach her the life of crime had his ex-wife not stolen her away and brainwashed Delaney against him. He had no doubt that she'd find that damn photo...or die trying.

****

John slid from beneath Delaney's arm and placed his pillow in the spot, leaving her something to snuggle with. He eased the door shut behind him as he headed into his kitchen in search of coffee. Last night had been amazing. She had been amazing. Any other woman would have been hysterical and in tears if they'd watched a house blow up, but not Delaney. It showed just how strong she was.

They'd both passed out from pure exhaustion, and he'd gotten some much-needed sleep. Sleep that didn't contain dreams of her being hurt. He knew what was coming next. When she woke up, she'd act differently, maybe even try to persuade him that he should leave her alone, but it wasn't happening. She was stuck with him. He'd see it to the end. Hopefully, then his dreams would stop.

John started the coffee maker and slipped into the shower to awaken his senses. He needed to be fully alert and his mind functioning so they could come up with another plan that kept them both alive while in search of the photo. Was the photo even real? John finished getting cleaned up and returned to the kitchen to find Delaney leaning against the counter, a full mug of coffee pressed to her lips. She was wearing one of his T-shirts and it hung to her knees.

"Sorry, I had to borrow this. I don't have anything to wear."

John walked over to her and pressed a kiss to her lips before he poured himself some coffee. "You're about the same size as my Aunt Claire. Why don't you get a shower and cleaned up? You can wear one of my shirts and the jeans you had on over there, and we'll raid her closet."

"Oh, John, I couldn't do that."

"She won't mind. She has more clothes than she knows what to do with."

As if on cue, his doorbell rang and he went to answer it. Standing on his porch was his mother, Aunt Claire, and Aunt Emma. His Aunt Claire had bags in her hands, his mother had bags from the restaurant, and his aunt Emma had two trays of coffee cups in carriers.

"Hope we didn't wake you." His mom smiled and pushed past him with her sisters right behind her.

"Come on in," he said after they'd already invaded his house and were heading to the kitchen.

Aunt Emma paused in passing. She winked and whispered, "We thought you could use a little help."

John followed them into the kitchen. If he was a woman, he might have shed a tear. He loved his family, and this was just another reason why. Rallying when the chips were down was one of their best qualities. They were like a unit taking charge. His Aunt Emma was passing out coffee. His mom had gone for the plates and started pulling out containers, opening them to reveal scrambled eggs, bacon, sausage, pancakes, and pastries. Aunt Claire had Delaney on her feet with her hand lifted to her side while she walked around her.

"We're about the same size. My clothes might be a little baggie for you, but..." She grinned. "I brought belts," Aunt Claire said in a singsong voice.

She cupped her hand around her mouth and whispered kind of loudly. "I didn't know what size your delicates are, so I brought a variety of different sizes with the tags still on."

"You keep a variety of new ones in sizes you don't wear?" Delaney asked, unable to keep the skepticism out of her voice.

"Of course, dear, one can never be too prepared, especially in our family."

"Okaaayyyy."

Aunt Claire shoved the bags into Delaney's hands before making a shooing motion. "Now go get cleaned up and changed; we'll keep your breakfast warm."

Delaney didn't move. She glanced around the room at everyone. "Why are you doing this? I'm a virtual stranger."

Her eyes grew misty with unshed tears. The need to comfort her overwhelmed him. He started to head toward her but was cut off by his mom. Abby reached her first.

Abby placed her palms on Delaney's arms. "Delaney, we're going to help you." She glanced back at John before turning around. "We're all going to help you. It's what we do."

John's heart felt full. His family was the best.

A loan tear slipped freely down Delaney's cheek, drawing John out of his thoughts.

"Excuse us." He reached for her and escorted her out of the kitchen and into his bedroom. He pressed a kiss to her forehead and winked. "They've taken a liking to you." He gave her a saucy grin. "Don't worry, they'll grow on you."

He left her in the bedroom and eased the door shut, returning to find his mother and aunts in the kitchen. They'd put the food in the stove to keep warm and were sitting at the table drinking coffee. He leaned against the doorway. "Thank you."

"Aw, honey. You don't need to thank us. She's like part of the family," his mom replied. She gestured to the chair next to hers. "Now, come sit down so we can figure out how to help you."

Sitting down, he picked up one of Emma's famous coffees and took a deep sip, letting the warm liquid coat his throat.

"Did you get anything off the dagger?" he asked.

"When I touched it, I zoned out and saw the actual killing. She was right; Ritchie Jessup was the one that plunged the knife into that man's body."

"Did you see any useful premonitions?"

Abby had her hands around her coffee cup. Her gaze held his. "I saw the photo being taken, and I saw something else."

"Really? What?"

"I saw Delaney's mom in the distance holding a video camera. I think there's more proof than just the photo. I think she got it on video too."

John's mouth parted. He turned to look at his Aunt Emma. "Any luck with the ghost?"

She shook her head. "She's still babbling and not making a bit of sense. We've started to keep a journal, so that once you tell Delaney our secret, we can show it to her and see if any of it means something to her."

"Have you told her?" Claire asked.

The idea of keeping secrets from her ate at his gut. The longer he withheld the truth, the less likely she'd ever trust him much less believe his claims. John shook his head. "I didn't trust her until recently. I haven't found the right time yet."

"If you want to keep her in your life, then don't wait too long, or it will be her that doesn't trust you," Emma added.

They chatted about the house, the insurance, and the family until Delaney joined them again. His mom and aunts dished out breakfast and they all sat down to eat. "How can we help? What do you need?" His mom asked.

Delaney paused, holding her fork in mid-air. "I'm afraid you can't unless you can tell me where Vinnie was staying so we can check out his place."

Claire smiled. John knew that smile. It was one of triumph.

"Is his last name Carmichael?"

Delaney's mouth parted. "How did you know?"

Claire shrugged. "Tight-knit community and I hear all of the gossip, dear. It doesn't hurt that Abby also figured it out."

"Well?" John asked, excitement filling his veins. He didn't have to question how either of them figured it out. All his mom would have to do was touch the body or something he owned and it was possible that she'd see the scene. And, well, his aunt Claire knew everything about everybody who stepped foot in their town. Though she had the ability to read the minds of others, she also liked to listen to gossip. If they could get to Vinnie's and find the photo, this could all be over by lunch.

"He rented the Hamptons' lake house."

John ate his breakfast in silence, letting his mind wander over the possibility of everything being over today. He wasn't ready to see her go, but if finding the photo meant keeping her alive, he'd rather have the photo than see her get hurt.

His mom and aunts all eased into conversation, pulling Delaney into the mix with questions that were non-evasive, trying to set her mind at ease.

"Isn't that right, John?"

John's gaze flew up upon hearing his name. "Huh? What?"

"You will bring Delaney to the Christmas party next week."

"Oh no, I couldn't," she protested.

"Sure you can," Abbey announced with a grin on her face. John's mom happily voicing her opinion was nothing unusual.

John laid his hand over Delaney's on the table. "It's a tradition and, besides, it's your fault I'm going to have to beat off women to prevent them from molesting me, thanks to the rumors you started."

"Rumors?" his mom asked.

Claire grinned. "Yeah, I've heard those too. I'll tell you all about it in the car."

When they were done eating and the kitchen cleaned, Claire laid her palm on Delaney's shoulder. "I have the perfect dress in mind for you. You're going to love it, and I won't take no for an answer. You're practically like family."

John walked his family outside to the SUV. "I appreciate your help with Delaney and the clothes."

"Aw, sweet pea, we'll always try and help." Aunt Emma hugged him before disappearing to the driver's side.

"I like her," Aunt Claire announced while hugging him. She paused to whisper in his ear. "She was going to run; I read it in her mind. She thinks she's bringing the danger to your door." She leaned back. "Don't let her get away."

Claire patted his arm before sliding into the vehicle.

"Sweetie." His mom lingered with her palms on his arm. She had something to say. She always had something to say. "This one isn't like the other girls."

"Mom, do we have to talk about this now?"

"I know you like this girl, but you have to keep your eye on the ball. Her father is trying to kill you." She reached up on her tiptoes and kissed his cheek. "She might not feel the same about you when you kick his ass."

John opened the passenger door and guided his mom inside. "You say the sweetest things."

She winked. "That's how I snagged your father. Now go work the Bennett charm. Help your dad and uncle catch this guy, and tell her how you feel."

John's lips parted but he remained speechless. Was it that obvious to everyone?

She rolled down the window. "Close your mouth, dear. Your feelings are written all over your face."

John snapped his mouth shut and rubbed his neck as he watched the three women, who helped raise him, back out of his driveway. He owed each of them his gratitude for helping his mom adjust to being a single parent. They each held a special place in his heart. They were wise beyond their years and their abilities.

"Are you going to stand out there all day?" Delaney called from behind him. He spun on his heels to find her leaning on the doorframe, her arms crossed over her chest.

"Women," he muttered beneath his breath, and then a grin formed on his lips. He ushered her back into the house and closed the door behind him.

"They sure are bossy."

"So are you." His lips twitched, John failed to hide the humor in the resemblance. "They can't help themselves, but they mean well."

John slung on his shoulder holster, checked the clips in his guns, and slid them in. He grabbed his jacket and keys and headed for the door. "How about a trip to the lake?"

"What about your dad and uncle? Won't they get mad at us for going to check it out?"

"Nah, we're saving them some leg work. If we find anything, we'll call it in. So, are you ready to go?"

Her eyes sparkled, but her enthusiasm was contradicted by the nervousness that went immediately to her stomach. "I thought you'd never ask."

She picked up her purse and walked out the front door.

CHAPTER 11

John eased down the dirt road, pulling into the drive in front of the Hamptons' lake house. Lights were on inside, yet he couldn't see a soul. "Why don't you stay here while I check it out?"

"As if." She slid out of the SUV before he had a chance to argue. "I might have to save you again. Besides, you don't know what you're looking for. I do."

John pulled out one of his guns, the grip tight in his hand. They walked to the door. Apprehension ate at his gut. He'd much rather do this alone and have Delaney behind the security walls at Tactical, but they were here. She was here and, because of that, he'd be cautious, more cautious than normal. John peered into the glass window next to the door. The lights were on and everything looked normal. There was no broken furniture, nothing ransacked. He surmised that they were one step ahead of the Jessups, or things would have looked much different.

"Should we knock?"

John shook his head and pulled out his wallet. He slipped out a credit card and headed for the door. "No."

"This is breaking and entering. We could get in trouble."

John paused, pulled out his phone, and fired off a text.

"Not any more. Aunt Claire will call and get it taken care of."

"Why didn't you call your uncle to get a warrant?"

"We'd waste too much time."

Delaney nodded while John returned his phone to his pocket and got back to the task of trying to pick the lock.

He slid his card into the jamb and was trying to work it free. There was a dead bolt he hadn't been anticipating. So he worked harder. Frustrated, he thought he might have to break it down when he heard the click and the door swung open. Delaney stood on the other side.

"The back door wasn't locked."

"That was careless of him."

"Easy exit, in case he had to run."

John slid his credit card into his pocket while following behind Delaney. The home was a typical lake house. Fireplace, couches, tables, and kitchen. John covered his mouth, a gag forming in his throat. "What is that smell?"

Delaney sniffed the air and her eyes widened. "Smells like soured milk."

They both walked into the kitchen and paused. The kitchen was nothing like the living room. A half-eaten pizza sat in the box. Half-empty cartons of orange juice and milk had been left out on the table. Newspapers were spread open, the fridge door was standing wide, and the sink was full of dishes that needed to be washed.

"Guess he won't be getting his security deposit back," Delaney whispered while glancing down at the moldy bread sitting on a plate.

John picked up the newspaper left open to the comics before tossing it back. His gaze fell on an open courtesy map of the lake that was given to visitors. Circles were drawn around surrounding boat slip storage areas. Did the guy have a boat?

"John," Delaney called from down the hall. She was standing outside of an office, her mouth parted.

He moved to stand next to her, his gaze going into the room, and now he knew why she was confused and staring. "I'll be a son of a bitch."

John stepped into the room. The walls were covered with photos of different locations throughout Southall. One of the bank, another of the coffee shop, the library, the police department. He recognized every structure in his hometown. He spun around to the wall behind him to find amateur photos of the lake and people on boats and some of the more picturesque places in town, including one of the Grove from the road.

Delaney walked into the room, plopped down in the chair behind the desk, and started opening drawers. He moved to stand behind her and watched as she pulled out a wallet, flipping it open.

A photo of the dead informant stared back. He was dressed in a business suit with his hair slicked back, his blue eyes alive with excitement. His name wasn't Vinnie as Delaney knew him to be; no, his name was Mark Drake. Next to that was a badge, and not just any badge, but one that John was all too familiar with. It was FBI.

"He was a Fed," she whispered as her hand flew to her mouth.

"Wouldn't your dad have known?"

He shook his head. "Not right away, not if he was deep under cover. He wouldn't have had an ID on him and they'd be looking under the alias. They still would have figured it out after running his prints but just not as quick."

"That might have been too late."

John slipped the wallet from her hand and let out a long, deep breath. This new revelation twisted his gut, making it difficult to breathe. Her father was deadly, strong enough to beat a man with the same training as John and his father. The implications stared him in the face. "Del, this isn't good. Where did you say you knew him from?"

Delaney leaned back in the chair, her gaze searching the pictures on the wall.

"I don't know." She shook her head. "It's all a blur. He had information on one of my stories. I thought I found him, not the other way around. Oh God."

"Del, I have to call this in." John pulled out his cell phone and called his father. If anyone knew what to do, his dad would.

"I need some air." Her hand covered her mouth as if she was about to be sick. "I'll wait for you outside."

Tears were shining in her eyes, and confusion clouded her face. He wanted to go to her, to hold her and tell her everything would be okay, but it wasn't. He had a duty to the fallen agent. He had a duty to let all of the others know. Within hours, other agents would arrive. Within days, Delaney and he would be questioned in detail about what they knew.

****

Delaney walked out the back door, her mind was reeling with the fact that she'd been played. Had the Fed been after her the entire time, or was he searching for the photo too? It didn't make sense. She rubbed at the goose bumps on her arms, the long shirt doing little to protect her from the December air. Her gaze was on the lake, but her mind was searching for answers, answers that only the dead could provide.

"I'm screwed," she whispered into the wind. Realization that she might never find the photo sank into her soul.

"Not yet, but you will be," a deep voice whispered in her ear as a hand clamped over her mouth and an arm wound around her waist, holding her tight. A tongue ran up her cheek.

She stiffened.

"That's right, Delaney. You're mine," Marco whispered in her ear, pressing his body against hers.

Delaney squirmed, trying to break his hold, but his fingers pressed into her skin painfully hard.

He jostled her body, pulling her back against him. "You aren't going anywhere."

She lifted her foot and came down hard on his toes. His grip loosened, and she'd almost gotten away, but his hand caught her wrist. His fist landed against her face, dropping her to her knees. Pain shot through her face, making her vision blur. She drew in a deep breath, knowing it might be her last.

She tried to stand, but he hit her again on the same side of the head. All of her strength vanished as she dropped to the ground.

"You aren't going anywhere." Marco kicked her twice in the ribs. She heard a loud crack and her breath whooshed from her body. She gripped her side, unable to move.

Marco leaned down next to her and pressed a knife to her throat. "I'm just getting started, baby."

He grabbed her hair, pulling painfully and bringing her to her feet. She struggled to keep her eyes from closing, her body wanting the rest, her mind not ready to give up. He pressed his back into her body, the knife painfully at her throat. "I'll finally show Ritchie who's the boss. Are you ready to die?"

Delaney noticed John out of the corner of her eye. He was peering around the house, the barrel of the gun trained on both of them.

"Are you?" she whispered. Her lips twitched into a knowing smile.

She balled her fist and using every bit of strength she had, nailed him in the groin. His hold instantly loosened, releasing her. Unable to stand, she collapsed back to the ground.

A shot rang out on the quiet lake. Marco dropped to the ground. His eyes were closed, his lifeless body unmoving. A single bullet hole had hit him dead center in his forehead.

Pain racked her body and her breathing became labored. The threat gone, John slid to his knees next to her. She was safe. John was with her and she was safe. She closed her eyes and let the darkness pull her under.

****

Delaney blinked her eyes open to the slow hum of the machines nearby. The sound of a constant blip—her heartbeat—filled the room. The smell of flowers drifted to her nose. She turned her head and found John sitting, sound asleep, in a hospital chair across the room. A tear slid over her cheek. He'd saved her, like the prince in a fairy tale. He'd rescued her more times than anyone in her life.

A hand gently squeezed hers from the other side of the bed. She turned to find John's mom standing there.

"He hasn't left your side, not once," she whispered in a quiet tone.

The news clenched her heart tight, breaking through some of the ice she'd used as a shield. "He looks like hell."

Abby chuckled. "You look worse. How do you feel?"

"Like I was used as a punching bag." Delaney tried to lift her hands to touch her face and winced at the pain in her chest.

Abby took her hand and eased it back down. "You were. You've got two cracked ribs, a black eye, and a concussion. I'd say the guy did a number on you."

"I fared better than him." Delaney tried to smile, but her face was too tender to move.

Pulling up a chair next to the bed, Abby sat. "There's something you should know about the Bennett men. They go all cavemen when the woman they love gets hurt."

Love? Did she just imply that John loved her? "Nooo, you've got it wrong. He's helping me so he can get rid of me, that's all."

Abby gave a small smile. "Well, I'll let you two work that out, but I know my son. He's a good man."

Delaney turned toward John, her mind replaying everything he'd done for her and to her since she'd arrived. She whispered, "The best."

She turned back to face John's mother. "I'm sorry for dragging him into this. You have to know I never intended to let him help. He kind of railroaded me."

Patting Delaney's hand, Abby smiled. "That's another annoying Bennett trait. Can I get you anything?"

"Not unless you know someone who can get me released. I hate hospitals."

Abby rose and grinned. "Just so happens I do." She walked to the door and tugged it open. "Just hang tight while we get this worked out."

"Thank you," Delaney replied before watching Abby disappear.

****

John lay with his eyes closed, afraid to move while eavesdropping over his mother's conversation with Delaney. He'd almost quit breathing when he heard his mom mention love. His first instinct had been to correct her, but now he wasn't sure. He'd watched Delaney get beat up and, with every blow, his anger rose and his heart ached. The thought of losing her became unacceptable. He waited until his mother left the room to stretch out his arms and blink his eyes open.

"Were you listening, Bennett?" Delaney accused.

"Not on purpose."

She turned to look at him. Her eyes were teary. "Thank you."

John stretched his arms over his head before standing and making his way to the bed. "You look like hell."

"Yeah, well, so do you. How many hours have I been in here?"

"Not hours, days. Two of them to be precise."

Delaney's eyes grew big. The move made her wince. "And you've been here all that time?"

He eased down onto the bed beside her and traced the hair around her face. His fingers were gentle, his actions caring. "Of course." He leaned down and pressed a gentle kiss to her lips. "We're in this together."

His mother and his Aunt Elizabeth came back into the room. "Okay, so here's the deal." Elizabeth approached the bed and held Delaney's gaze. "I'm still waiting on some of your blood work, but I'm going to release you into John's care on one condition."

"Condition?" Delaney glanced at John before turning back to Elizabeth. "What's the condition?"

"I've been brought up to speed on everything that's going on. These guys are going to continue to chase you, and I don't want you to make yourself a target until you heal."

"I can't stop them from coming after me, so I don't understand." Delaney's confusion clouded her face.

"Well, that's the great part." Aunt Elizabeth grinned. "As long as you're in town, they'll keep trying. So I'm giving you the option of leaving town or staying in the hospital until you recuperate."

She shook her head. "I can't leave."

Abby stepped up and placed her hand on Delaney's. "Sure you can." She looked up at John and her eyes twinkled with a hint of mischief and concern. "John and you are going to stay at our beach house in Florida for the week. Where you can relax and heal and John can help."

John's lips twitched, he was unable to hold in his smile. "Brilliant."

"What? No! We can't leave. I have to find the photo."

"Delaney, it's only for one week. It will give us time to regroup and for you to heal. Ritchie doesn't know where the photo is. He's waiting for you to find it." He shrugged. "When he can't find you, maybe he'll give up and leave."

Abby nodded as if confirming his thoughts. She announced, "I'll have the family jet ready and you can leave within the hour." Abby pulled out her phone and started walking toward the door, not giving Delaney any time to argue.

Four hours later, and after he'd given Delaney a lot of reassurance that the trip was what she needed, the airplane touched down at the private airport. John breathed a sigh of relief for the first time since meeting her. Ritchie wouldn't even believe she'd left for Florida, much less be able to find her in the touristy town in the Panhandle that was currently running amuck with snowbirds. They wouldn't have to look over their shoulder for any unseen threat. There was no way anyone could have followed them while flying.

John scooped Delaney's fragile body up into his arms and cradled her against his chest, careful of her broken ribs as he prepared to carry her off the plane. Her black eye had started turning an ugly shade of purple with spots of a mustard yellow color.

"You can put me down. My legs aren't broken."

"No, just everything else is." John disembarked and headed toward the waiting SUV. One of Tactical Maneuvers' operatives was holding the door open. He handed John the keys. "The house has been stocked and the security has been checked. You should enjoy an uneventful stay."

John smiled down at Delaney's doubtful face.

He helped her into the passenger seat and strapped the seatbelt over her. He placed a tender kiss on her lips. "I'm just going to get our luggage. Hang tight."

She gave a small nod; he returned moments later, sliding into the driver's seat. "You're going to love it here."

"Hmm," was her only reply as she turned her gaze to the window and watched the sun setting beyond the dunes as he drove up Front Beach Road.

The roads were empty save for the elderly drivers with the northern license plates. There was no sign of spring breakers or locals on the beach. The peace and quiet would be good for both of them. No relatives, no dagger, no Ritchie. It was just Delaney and John for one full week in the small beach town.

A group of motorcycles passed, going in the opposite direction, holding men and women clad in leather jackets and jeans. Panama City was a military town situated in the Panhandle of Florida. It catered to the Air Force base and Navy and always managed to draw back a few veterans once they retired. His family had visited the beach every summer, including the one when his mom met his father. These very same white sands were where John was conceived.

John grinned at the thought. He might not be ready to start a family, but he'd enjoy getting to know Delaney in a relaxed state. The stress of the last couple of weeks was playing hell on her body and her mind.

****

Delaney couldn't believe she was in Florida. It wasn't a vacation, but she'd always wanted to go, just never in her current condition. She'd dreamed of having a beach wedding, if she ever got married. John took a scenic route full of high-rise hotels with empty parking lots. Every few hundred yards, there was a break in the concrete structures, and she could see a long stretch of beach. The white sand was the color of flour, and the color of the ocean bore a resemblance to John's turbulent blue eyes. Seagulls flew above the water, dipping down to catch their meals. The place was beautiful, even if the reason she was here was anything but.

She must be the only female on earth whose father had repeatedly tried to kill her; although the last attack she wasn't so sure about. Marco had mentioned it was out of personal revenge for him. Daddy dearest was going to be pissed off that his second-in-command had tried to take the reins, had tried to kill her before finding the photo. He'd be seething when he finally figured out that Marco was dead.

It took another thirty minutes before they made it to the opposite end of the beach. The beach houses were spread farther apart, and what few cars she'd seen had disappeared, giving her the illusion that the beach wasn't the tourist attraction she'd imagined. John turned into a cul-de-sac, taking them even closer to the beach. There was an iron gate blocking their entry. John handed an ID to the guy and waited for the gate to lift. The burly guy at the gate nodded. "It's been a while since you visited."

"It's been too long, Shawn." John took his ID back and tossed it into the console between them. "Listen, I'd like the block on lockdown and, if there's any sign of trouble, I want to be notified immediately."

Shawn straightened his stance. His lips pulled into a fine line. "I'll double security while you're here. There won't be any trouble."

"Thanks." John nodded and pulled through the security gate that seemed to cut them off from the rest of the town.

"My family owns all of these homes and the security is pretty tight."

"I would say so but, honestly, I don't think Ritchie will find us here."

John shrugged. "Even if he does, he'll have to get past the two Navy SEALs and four Tactical Maneuvers security operatives patrolling the perimeter, including the beach. I'm not taking any chances while we're here. I want you to be able to relax in peace while you heal." He shot her a panty-melting grin that included dimples. "Doctor's orders."

"So, no beach sex, huh?" She laughed at her own question. The movement jarred her body and made her wince. She steeled herself and drew in a long breath to ride through the pain. The medication Elizabeth had prescribed to help with the pain was starting to wear off.

"Not this time."

"All I want is to take a nice long, hot bath and to wash my hair. I don't need much more than that."

John pulled up to the largest house within the semi-circle. The white, two-story house had blue shutters and a wrap-around porch. She could see the ocean from the driveway. "It's beautiful."

He parked and turned off the SUV. "Wait here so I can help you."

She opened the door, not waiting, and slid out of her seat until her feet touched the ground. He was frowning when he reached her. "I said to wait."

"I'm not an invalid, John. I can walk...just not very fast."

Delaney clutched her side, as if to hold it in place, as she took the front porch steps one at a time. Even with John supporting her elbow, the move still hurt. He punched a set of numbers into the security pad and placed his palm on the plate.

"Hey, did you ever figure out how they broke into the Grove with all of your security?"

John held the door open and helped her across the threshold. "My dad is reviewing the footage. All I can think of is that they cut down the entire system. That would have been the only way that the alarms didn't go off."

She gave a slow nod. "I guess you guys need a backup that won't go down so easily."

He ushered her toward a room in the back, not even letting her take in the beautiful décor. "Actually, my dad hardly uses the Grove. When he married my mom, he built her a new house next to my aunt's. It's complete with guards, security checkpoints, and a host of other security measures."

"Then why didn't he sell?" she asked while watching John grab a towel and start the bath water.

"The same reason you didn't sell your mom's, I suppose. It held too many memories." John grabbed a travel kit from beneath the sink. "This has everything you should need to get you started. I'm going to grab the luggage and find us something to make for dinner. I'm sure you're starving by now."

Delaney smiled. "Thank you." She pushed the door closed behind him and peeled her clothes off, letting them fall to the floor. She glanced at her reflection in the mirror and froze. She reached for the swollen black-and-blue area and gingerly touched her flesh. She was a train wreck; she looked like death warmed over. The rest of her face was pale white, as though it hadn't seen the light of the sun since she'd started her quest. Her good eye was bloodshot with a large bag beneath it. Her lips were pale, and she'd lost weight. Her hair was oily and slicked back into a ponytail.

She looked like a stranger, even to herself. This wasn't the person she was. This wasn't how her mother would want her to be. The photo was important, but so was her life, and right now, it appeared she was knocking on death's door.

A tear fell over the purple bruise, and her heart felt squeezed as though it was being gripped in an invisible vise. Delaney let herself cry, a real cry for the first time since her mother died. Her shoulders sagged, and she dropped her head, wrapping her fingers in a death grip on the sink. The tears came fast and hard, falling off her face in huge drops. She didn't want this. She didn't want it for herself, and John didn't deserve this.

The running water camouflaged her sobs. She was done feeling sorry for herself. That wasn't her either. She was a fighter, damn it, not some child who needed her hand held.

She straightened her shoulders and nodded at her reflection. She could handle this; she *would* handle this.

The steam from the bath started to rise, and she leaned over turning the water it off. She peeled off the bandage from around her ribs. Her entire side was covered in black and blue, but with the bandage gone, so was the restriction on her lungs. She grabbed the travel kit and laid it on the side of the bath before she stepped in and eased down into the hot water. A lengthy sigh left her lips as she let the warmth soak into her skin, pulling her from the pity party she'd been having. The water felt refreshing against her skin, the dirt and grime easy to wash away. Washing her hair had been difficult with the use of only one arm. She tried to raise the other one over her head, and the pain took her breath away. She'd manage with one hand because there was no way in hell she'd be asking John to help her.

CHAPTER 12

John stood outside the bathroom door with his hand on the knob. He'd heard her crying, and every fiber of his being wanted to comfort her. He listened intently as the water shut off, and then he heard the tiny splash she made while climbing into the tub. He was one gasp away from going to help her when he heard her sigh. He released the breath he'd been holding and took a step back. She was okay. They were both okay, he reminded himself. He heaved the suitcase that Aunt Claire had packed onto the bed. She'd been quick at packing items she thought Delaney might need. His mother had packed his and met him at the airport with both bags. He slid the suitcase open so it would be one less thing for her to worry about and left it on the bed for easy access.

He walked into the kitchen and scoured the cabinets and fridge for something easy and quick to fix. He settled on the plump steaks in the fridge just waiting to be prepared. He said a silent thank you to whoever had done the shopping and anticipated they would need something already thawed. He grabbed veggies from the fridge to make a salad to go with the steak and set everything out before walking outside to start the grill. He'd just thrown the steaks on to cook when he spotted her in the living room. Her gaze held his through the French doors. He smiled; she frowned.

He closed the cover on the grill and walked back inside. "Everything okay?"

"Yeah." Her frown slid into a small smile, but even the small smile was better. "This place suits you."

"Come keep me company while I grill." He gestured over his shoulder to the back patio. "The chairs out there are padded so you can rest."

She followed him outside and eased down into one of the lounge chairs, crossing her legs at the ankles. Her body looked more relaxed, but her eyes looked heavy. He breathed in the salty air and turned back to flip the steaks.

"I can't believe it's not cold here in December."

John closed the lid again and plopped down on a chair near the glass table. He lifted his beer to his lips for a long pull. "They still have a couple months before it gets cold and, even then, it's nothing like the weather in North Carolina."

****

"I've only ever dreamed of living in a place like this." The fresh, salty air helped ease all of her senses. The tide breaking on the beach was an easy sound she could fall asleep to. This trip had been what she needed, even if it wasn't an official vacation.

John's phone vibrated against the glass table. He checked the caller ID before answering.

"Hey, Aunt Elizabeth, is everything okay?"

Delaney listened to the one-sided conversation.

"Yeah, we got in just a little bit ago."

John's earlier smile slipped.

"Uh...sure." John walked over to Delaney and handed her the phone. "She wants to talk to the patient."

"To me?" Delaney whispered.

"Yeah, I'm sure she's just checking in on you."

Delaney tried to stand and John helped her. "Hello."

"Hi, Delaney, do you have a minute?"

She glanced over her shoulder and saw John checking the steaks.

"Yeah. I'm following doctor's orders."

"Good." She heard the woman laugh. "You're the first. Most of the Bennetts just do whatever the hell they please."

"Well, good thing I'm not a Bennett."

"Listen, can you excuse yourself from John? There are some things we need to discuss. I didn't want to do it over the phone but, seeing as you're several states away, I didn't think it could wait."

The hair on the nape of her neck stood up. Goosebumps peaked on her arms. "Sure, let me just go to the bedroom."

Delaney took a nervous breath and walked into the bedroom closing the door behind her. She eased down onto the bed and waited, not knowing what could possibly be wrong.

"I'm alone."

"Delaney, I don't know how to tell you this."

"Just spill it, Doc; it can't be that bad." Delaney's heart was racing in her chest. The unknown always scared the hell out of her. This call, out of the blue, wasn't going to be a good thing; she could feel it in her bones.

She listened as John's Aunt Elizabeth took a deep breath. "I just want you to understand that I abide by doctor-patient confidentiality."

"Uh, okay."

"We got your blood work back."

"And?"

"You're pregnant."

Delaney's mouth fell open and her vision blurred as tears brimmed in her eyes. She couldn't have heard her right. "You must be mistaken. I'm on birth control."

"Not all birth control is infallible."

Delaney's head drooped forward and she clenched her eyes closed. This couldn't be happening to her, not now. Not when she was being chased by a maniac.

"Delaney, I have to ask...is the baby John's?"

"Yes." The answer came out a whisper. "You aren't going to tell him, are you?"

"No, but he deserves to know. Let me give you a little story about my nephew that I'm not sure he's shared with you yet."

The last thing Delaney wanted to listen to was a story, not with the newest turmoil going on in her head. But she listened anyway.

"His father was in the witness protection program when he met Abby. From what I understand, it was love at first sight. She gave him her virginity, and he got her pregnant, but then he disappeared. She and her family searched for him for years so she could tell him that he had a son. It wasn't until John was eighteen, when the same serial killer his father was hiding from had his sights set on Abby, that his father reentered their life."

Delaney's heart ached for John as a little boy without a father to look up to.

"My point is, I'm asking you, please don't do that to him. He deserves to know and be a part of his child's life.

"I know you two have to work things out, and there are things about his family and him that he needs to tell you, so why don't you use this week to really open up to each other? Get to know one another, even if as nothing more than friends. You owe it to yourself and to the baby. John really is a good guy. He's one of the best, and he won't let you down."

Delaney heard John calling her from the living room, and she jumped from the bed, remembering too late that she shouldn't have. Her stomach turned from the sudden movement as she tried to breathe through the nausea.

"Thank you for calling. John's looking for me and I need to go."

"You can't take any more of the pain meds I sent with you. They'll hurt the baby. You need to stick to *Tylenol* for now, until we get you checked out. When you get back, we need to see about scheduling an appointment for you. I can make a few calls if you'd like. You really should start taking some prenatal vitamins but, since it's still early in the game, I guess that can wait a week."

"Thank you. I have to go."

Delaney disconnected the call, not even waiting on Elizabeth to answer. Her hand went to her stomach as bile rose in her throat. She swallowed down the apprehension that was clawing her throat and walked out of the room to find John hovering over the dinner table. He placed a large salad in the middle of the table and the steaks and baked potatoes were already on the plates. "Dinner's ready." He straightened. "Is everything okay? Did my aunt say something to upset you?"

"I'm fine. The food looks great." Delaney placed a fake smile on her lips and tried to change the topic. She pushed the fact she was pregnant to the back of her mind. She needed time to digest the information and figure out what she was going to do. The thought of telling John made her stomach roll.

John pulled out her chair and helped her ease into it before he fixed her a side salad for her plate. She watched him, taking in everything she'd noticed before and more. John was a good guy. He was sexy, smart, and he had a good heart. If she'd been baby-daddy shopping, he would have fit the bill, but she wasn't.

John placed a beer down in front of her. That small gesture made the pregnancy seem real. "Can I have some water instead?"

"Sure." John didn't even bat a lash at her request, just filled a glass and placed it in front of her before sitting down. He sat across from her in the soft candlelight. The flicker from the flame danced around the dimly lit room.

"I made both steaks a medium. I wasn't sure how you liked yours and you'd disappeared."

"Medium is great," she replied and didn't give an explanation for her absence.

He took a bite of his steak, yet his gaze remained focused on her. She could tell he had something on his mind, even though her news was probably bigger. Life-altering huge. What would he do? He had goals and dreams that didn't include her. What would he think about a baby?

"How about, after dinner, we go lie down and talk? There are some things I need to tell you."

A bubble of laughter slipped from her lips, and her hand flew to her mouth. Her eyes widened at her slip. "Sorry, there are some things I have to tell you too."

He nodded. Tension filled the air between them now. They ate with idle chitchat. John mostly talked about his family and the times they'd spent on the beach, as if he was her tour guide. She spoke of her mother and what it was like growing up. The conversation skirted around why they were both there and the threat that awaited their return, not to mention her own little secret.

They finished eating and adjourned to the bedroom. She changed into one of the nightgowns Claire had packed, and he ditched his jeans and left on his boxers. They both slid under the covers. She was hyper aware of his body pressed against hers. He treated her with gentle hands, making sure she was comfortable before he let himself lie back.

"I would hold you, but I don't want to hurt you."

"That's okay. You said you had something you wanted to tell me?"

John was quiet in the stillness of the room. He took a deep breath and rolled onto his side, propping his head in his palm. "Delaney. You know I have dreams about you."

She nodded. His big hand rested lightly on her stomach.

"And you know when my Uncle Mike touched you that he knew what happened to us."

"Yeah, you never did explain how he knew."

"Well...my mother comes from a lineage of gifted people. Every one of the Bennetts, who share her blood, is gifted in some way or another."

"Everyone has dreams?" Delaney asked, unsure where the conversation was headed.

"No, I'm the only one with dreams. My mom has psychometry. She can touch an object and, in her mind, she's taken back in time to something significant about that item."

Delaney remained quiet, letting the information sink in.

"My Aunt Claire can read minds, although she'd never poke around without permission. My Aunt Lydia, whom you haven't met, can see into the future. She's probably the strongest of the bunch, but my Aunt Emma has two abilities."

"Oh?" Delaney asked, her mind trying to understand what he was talking about.

"Yes, she gets PMS-like symptoms when one of the family members is in trouble, and she can see ghosts."

Delaney tried to sit up to look at John and winced from the pull on her side. She took a deep breath and lay back down, trying to concentrate around the pain. Her hand went to her stomach, bringing back the conversation she'd had with Elizabeth and wondering just how long it would be before the others knew. Crap, she had a Bennett inside of her. What if her baby had some sort of ability too?

"You don't seem surprised. Say something."

"I've never met anyone with those abilities but, with all of the paranormal shows on television, I can't say I'm surprised. I'm just....hell, I don't know what I am," she conceded. She'd have to let all of that information simmer to make sense. "Why didn't you tell me before now?"

John lay back down and clasped his fingers beneath his head. "You're a reporter, and I had to make sure I could trust you with the information. If word got out about any of us, it could ruin more than careers. It could ruin our lives."

Delaney rolled onto her uninjured side and tossed her arm over his chest. She needed the closeness for what she had to tell him.

"John." Her voice came out a whisper, and he wrapped his arm beneath her head easing her further into his side.

His phone vibrated on the nightstand. "Hold that thought." He reached for it and checked the caller ID. He eased his arm from beneath her and sat up. "Hey, Aunt Emma, is everything okay?"

He glanced back at Delaney. "Yeah, I told her. She knows."

Delaney could hear the woman talking quickly on the other end of the phone. John leaned back against the pillow and laid his arm over his eyes. "Okay, we'll be home at the end of the week. Call me if you get anything else."

John tossed the phone back onto the nightstand and pulled Delaney back into his side. He reached for her necklace and lifted it off her chest. "You know how I told you my Aunt Emma could see ghosts…"

"Yeah." She wasn't sure she liked where this was headed.

He let the pendent rest on her chest. "Well, your mom showed up and was panicked."

"What!" Delany tried to sit up before he pulled her back to his side. "Calm down. All Emma could make out was that your necklace was the key. Do you have any idea what she was talking about?"

"No." She shook her head, her mind racing with what that could mean. Her mom had given her the necklace when she'd turned sixteen. It was precious to her and had been handed down through generations. That was all she knew about its origins. "Maybe your mom can touch it and see if she gets anything off of it."

"That's a great idea." John kissed Delaney's head and snuggled her in closer. "I told her we'd be back in a week. When we get back, I'll search for the photo. I don't want you getting hurt anymore."

"John, I'm not fragile."

"I know, Delaney, but we've had too many close calls. I don't want you hurt."

"I'm not going to be hurt." She slid out of his arms. "You aren't railroading me, Bennett. It's my necklace, my family, and my problem. I shouldn't have gotten you involved to begin with."

"Fine, but we do this smart. You stick by my side. Okay?" He pulled her back into his arms.

"Fine," she answered back.

"What did you want to tell me?"

The news she was going to tell him wouldn't leave her lips. If he knew she was pregnant, he'd try to insist she couldn't go after the photo. Hell, he'd probably want her to stay at the beach house. Maybe keeping that little bit of news to herself couldn't hurt for a few more days. Her mother's murderer would be brought to justice if it was the last thing she did. She would be more careful. She wouldn't leave his side until this was over. She had a duty, not only to herself, but to their unborn child, to keep them both safe. "It can wait."

****

The remainder of the week went by quickly. Her body was feeling better, and the pain was gone, even though the bruises remained. She'd used the time to get closer to John, to really see what type of person he was. She felt bad about keeping the secret from him but was going to wait until Abby touched her necklace. She'd decided if his mom didn't get a premonition, or whatever the heck she got from a single touch, then she was going to tell him and let the chips fall where they may. She needed to be certain she'd exhausted every means necessary before giving up the hunt. She had a future to figure out; it was just a matter of whether John wanted to be a part of it.

The flight back to Southall seemed longer than the trip to Florida. Maybe it was the anticipation of finding out where the photo was or the anxiety over telling John about the baby. The plane landed on the tarmac with a couple of bumps before she heard the down throttle of the engines as the plane began to slow, ultimately turning around. She felt every bump on the uneven pavement until the plane came to a complete stop. The flight attendant opened the door and gestured for them to disembark. Delaney stopped at the top of the stairs. Waiting below, next to the Tactical Maneuver SUV, were Claire and Abby. Claire could read minds. It wouldn't be long before the entire Bennett clan, including John, knew about the baby.

John eased her down the steps with a hand planted on her back. Delaney started reciting the alphabet in her head. As Delaney approached, Claire made a funny face. "I understand he told you."

Delaney nodded, trying not to lose her place in the alphabet sequence.

"I didn't mean to pry. I was just trying to see what I could do to help."

Delaney smiled. "I appreciate everything you've done, but I'd appreciate it if you'd let me keep my thoughts to myself."

"Of course, dear." Claire smiled. "I'll stay out of your head."

"Thank you."

"John, under the circumstances, I think it best if Delaney and you stay at either Claire's or my house until this is resolved. Your home isn't very safe."

"I agree." He glanced down at Delaney before meeting their gazes. "If it's all the same to you, I think we'll stay at Claire's. Delaney doesn't really know dad and you, yet. I think she'd be more comfortable being some place familiar."

Abby's lips slipped into a frown, disappointment evident on her face. Would she be disappointed knowing she would soon be a grandmother?

"Well, let's get you two over there, and then maybe we can figure out what is going on with your mom and the necklace."

Delaney's stomach flipped. It wasn't that she didn't believe and trust these people, but the possibility that at least one of them was hearing from her mom made her head swim and her heart ache. She'd give anything to talk to her mom just one last time. John loaded the luggage and, before she knew it, she was being whisked away again in an SUV with John sitting at her side. His Aunt Claire was chatting in the front seat about her plans for the big Christmas party that was scheduled for the next night, one that Delaney was dreading to attend. Her stomach rolled while butterflies fought in her belly. Her body ached, and her mind was one big ball of mess. She reached up and palmed her pendant, hoping that her mom would give her the strength to get through the surprises life kept throwing her way.

"You okay?" John whispered, leaning into her side.

Delaney flashed him a smile and nodded. Her clutch on the pendant dropped and she laced her fingers in her lap. She had to tell him; he deserved to know. She was praying that his mom could shed some light on the pendant and this would be over before she revealed her life-changing secret.

"Maybe we'll get the answers today." John's hand landed on her knee and he squeezed.

"Hopefully," she answered before turning her gaze to the window and watching the scenery in John's hometown. Would she live here with the baby? Let their child grow up in the same environment John had? Anything would be better than her younger years of being groomed by criminals.

CHAPTER 13

John dropped Delaney's and his bags in the foyer of Aunt Claire's house. He slid his hand around Delaney's and followed his mom and aunt toward the voices in the kitchen. His dad, Uncle Butch, and Uncle Mike were seated around the table which was covered with photos. Mike had one in his hand. "Yep, that's Ritchie all right." He tossed it back onto the table. "I'm surprised he got his hands dirty this time."

"Maybe he was careless," Uncle Butch replied.

John's dad shook his head. "Nope, not this guy. He only ever gets his hands dirty when it's personal and, even then, he doesn't normally leave evidence behind."

His mom strolled over to him and wrapped her arms around his neck while planting a kiss on his cheek. "Well, if he never leaves evidence behind, then how do you know it was him doing the deeds?"

"Due to witnesses who are too scared to talk and always disappear. We haven't been able to nail him yet. Until now."

John watched as Delaney picked up one of the photos of her father with Marco as they hid in the Grove. The photo depicted the blurred shape of an SUV in the distance on the road. The bastards were still there when they'd walked inside. The asshole had tried to kill his own damn daughter.

John balled his fist in an attempt to control his anger. He wanted to pound the asshole.

"What do we do now?"

Mike rose and scooped up the photos, taking back the one Delaney had in her hand. "We track down the son of a bitch and arrest him for arson and attempted murder."

"Arson and attempted murder. He did murder. He murdered my mother." Delaney's demanded.

John placed his arm around her shoulder. "They don't have any proof about your mom, but don't worry, Del. They'll pick him up for the other things and it will be enough to hold him and buy us some time to find the photo so we can really stick it to him."

The rising tension in her shoulders eased the longer he stood near her. She looked up and held his gaze. "We have to find that photo."

"I'll call when we find him," Mike called over his shoulder as he left the room.

Delaney lifted the locket over her head and walked over to John's mom, holding it out. "Mrs. Bennett?"

"My mom was Mrs. Bennett. You can call me Abby, dear." Abby took the necklace, closed her eyes, and clutched it tightly to her chest.

His mom swayed on her feet, rocking back and forth. "I'm in a room. A small room, watching a woman. She's frantically searching. Clothes are flying over her head as she throws them from the closet. Shoes and shoe boxes are thrown as she's digging for something."

"Where's the room?" Claire asked.

"I don't know yet," Abby said, her eyes still closed, her body still swaying. "The woman stopped. She picked up a jewelry case and set it down in front of her on the small bed."

John watched Abby tilt her head. "It's a wooden box and pieces of it move. The bottom front slides to the left leaving a gap for the wood on the right side to pull away. She tipped the box over. Delaney's locket slid out."

Delaney clenched John's hand. They were both hanging on every word.

"The wood around the jewelry box slides forward and one of the wood slats drops down, revealing the hidden key hole."

They watched as Abby leaned down trying to get a closer look. "It's the same shape as the pendant. She aligned it in the slot and pushed, and then the top of the box sprung open."

"What's she doing now?" John asked, adrenaline running through his body. He was ready to find the box. He was ready for this all to be over.

"She placed an envelope inside and locked it back up. But she didn't hide the key again. She kept it out. She put the box back together and placed it in the bottom of the closet.

"Is there a window in the room? Can you tell where you are?"

"A small window." Abby started walking across the room, and they frantically worked to move chairs and other things out of her path to avoid pulling her out of the scene.

Abby gave a quick intake of breath, and her hand flew to her mouth. Her eyes popped open, and she shook her head as if clearing the images.

"Well?" John asked, unable to hide his urgency. "What did you see outside the window?"

Abby handed the locket to Delaney. "I saw the lake."

Delaney's eyes widened. A look of excitement beamed in her eyes. "*The Rose.* I don't know why I didn't think of it sooner."

John held up his hand. "The rose?" He turned to his mom. "Isn't that the same word that Lily told us when we were trying to figure out who Delaney was in the beginning?"

Abby nodded. "Yeah, that's what Lily said. We just didn't know who or what it meant."

"Not who...what. *The Rose* is a boat. It was my grandmother's boat and the only place my dad didn't know about. Grandmother left it to my mom. I can't believe it's in Southall." Delaney spun around toward John. "We have to go." She hooked the necklace around her neck and grabbed John's hand, practically pulling him from the kitchen. "We have to go, now."

"Wait," Abby hollered as she hurried to follow. "I'm going with you,"

"Mom, you don't have to do this."

"Oh hell, yes I do. Two guns are better than one. Ritchie already tried to kill both of you. He won't get that chance again."

Delaney wasn't waiting and John didn't have time to argue with his mom. He just nodded and followed Delaney back out to the same SUV they'd arrived in.

****

John parked in front of the building that maintained the boat slips for the owners.

There were only three on the lake, and they had a one in three shot that this was the right one. If it wasn't, they'd check the other two. He was going to pull the door open to ask the office if Delaney's mom had registered one when he heard Delaney scream.

"It's right there," she said, pointing. "That is *The Rose*."

Delaney hurried down the dock and stopped in front of a red-and-black-painted boat. *The Rose* was scrolled in bold print along the back plank. "My mom only brought me here once, when we were on the run from my dad, but she used to tell me stories about her dad taking her on the boat when she was a little girl."

John helped Delaney and his mom on board before following behind them. The boat gently rocked in an easy motion against the ripples in the water. The moon lit the night sky and the stars twinkled above. It would be a beautiful night if it weren't for the elephant they were dealing with. The potential evidence to take down a killer was within reach.

Delaney jiggled the handle on the door that would take them below deck and turned around in dismay. "It's locked."

Abby patted her shoulder and pulled a hairpin from her hair. "No, sweetie." She eased Delaney to the side. "You just don't have the right key."

John couldn't help the smile that formed on his lips as his mom picked the lock, giving them the entrance they needed.

"Ah yes, here we are." Abby rose and pushed the door open, letting Delaney enter first. She hurried down the steps and into the small bedroom. She went into the closet and pulled out the wooden box that John's mom had described. They watched as she opened the jewelry box as if she'd done it a million times before.

"My mom used to let me play with this when I was little and, then one day, it just disappeared. I never knew where it went."

Delaney pulled the center portion out, revealing the hidden slot for the key. She lifted the pendant from around her neck, aligned it in place, and pushed down. The top sprung open just as his mom had said. Delaney reached in and pulled out a manila envelope before setting the box aside. She tore it open and dumped the contents onto the bed. Staring up at them, in a glossy finish, was Ritchie Jessup with his foot on top of a dead body. The dagger in his hand was dripping blood, and the son of a bitch was smiling. Next to that was a DVD in a plastic case. The word insurance was written on the outside.

Delaney looked up and held Mike's gaze. "It's over. It's finally over."

John pulled her into his arms and held her tight. Her body trembled in his arms, and his shirt dampened from her fresh tears.

His mom picked up the photo and the DVD then pulled the phone from her pocket. "We need to get these to the station, and I need to call your dad." She walked over to the steps and paused. "Come on you two. This isn't over until the evidence is safe. Right now, we're sitting ducks."

John rubbed up and down Delaney's arms and leaned out of her hold. "You okay?"

She nodded her eyes glassy with tears.

"We have to go." John used the pad of his thumb to wipe away a stray tear that fell. "I'm sorry, baby. But we really do have to go."

She nodded and inhaled a deep breath. "Let's go give your uncle the nail for Ritchie's coffin."

"That's my girl."

They followed Abby up the stairs and off the boat and got back into the SUV. His mom and he scanned the area. They both knew the threat wasn't over. Ritchie hadn't been picked up. John was glad his mom had come with them. He was glad to have the additional gun power, and he was glad they'd found what they needed. Delaney would be safe from the bastard once and for all.

They rode in complete silence to the police station. His nerves wouldn't relax until they turned the photo into evidence. His mom put them in a conference room and told them to wait, only to return moments later with John's dad and Uncle Mike on her heels while she carried in a laptop.

They put the DVD in, and they all sat in silence as they watched the scene on the screen. The dead man from the photo was on his knees, begging for his life.

"Do you recognize him?" John asked."

She slowly nodded. "I've seen him in pictures but I never knew who he was."

They all turned their attention back to the video. Marco hit the guy in the head, making him collapse against the ground. Ritchie kicked him until he was on his back, then pulled the dagger out his jacket, and shoved it into the man's chest.

The guy on the ground was still moving; the blow wasn't fatal. He could have possibly survived. The thought crossed John's mind while he watched in horror as Ritchie pulled out a gun and shot the man through the heart.

Delaney's hand flew over her mouth, and she turned into his chest. John ran his fingers through her hair, doing his best to support her while she watched the proof and what the the video actually meant. Her own flesh and blood, the man that was responsible for her coming into this world, was worse than a killer. He was a monster.

The DVD played on for a second longer and they watched as one of the other gang members snapped a picture. The computer screen filled with snow.

"Well, I think that's enough to convict."

John's father patted Delaney's shoulders. "You've done well. You've accomplished what the FBI has been trying to do for years."

She looked up at John. "Can we go?"

"Yes." He glanced over at his mom. "You got this?"

"Yeah, baby, I've got this. Why don't you take her to Claire's? You two have had a long day."

John tucked Delaney into his side. Her shoulders were slumped, and any energy she'd had before had drained. "Uncle Mike, you'll let us know when you pick him up?"

"Of course." He held the door open. "I'm going to make sure you get a police escort home, just in case."

"Thanks."

****

The ride back to Aunt Claire's was uneventful. Delaney remained quiet with her head propped against the window. She looked frail, but he couldn't blame her. Her mother was dead; her father was a murderer; and now, whom did she have? No one but him.

Claire was waiting for them on the porch, her arms wrapped around her waist.

Uncle Butch was standing beside her with his arm protectively over her shoulders. Claire had barely waited for the SUV doors to open before she was down the stairs and pulling Delaney into her arms. She ushered her inside. Butch placed his hand on John's shoulder, stopping him from following.

"We need to talk," Butch said. His gaze followed the retreating backs up the stairs.

"Can it wait?"

"No, but don't worry. Aunt Claire will take care of her."

John rubbed his neck and followed Uncle Butch into the kitchen. His uncle pulled out two beers and gestured for John to have a seat. This was the last thing he wanted to do. He needed to comfort Delaney. Her need for him was much more important than whatever Butch needed to tell him. But he owed his uncle, so he'd give him a few minutes.

John twisted the top off the beer and took a long pull. The amber liquid felt good going down his throat. The stress from the day eased out of his shoulders.

"You did well today."

"I didn't do anything."

"That's not how the FBI is going to see it. They're going to want you back. They may even throw incentives your way to get you to come work for them."

"Uncle Butch, can't this wait?"

He shook his head and took a gulp of his own beer. "John, you have to make a choice. You know that, right?"

"A choice about what?"

"The girl or the job."

"Why can't I have both?" John rose out of his chair; the move was challenging.

Butch rose. "We all like Delaney. We like her a lot. She's got spunk; she's smart; and she'd be good for you. But the FBI isn't going to like her past."

"Fuck them."

"John, you're throwing away the only dream you've had growing up. If you stay with her, it could ruin your career. I'm just warning you."

John placed the bottle on the table and patted his uncle's shoulder as he passed. "I know you're only trying to help, but I'm not ready to let her go."

Butch nodded, and John went in search of the woman who held his dreams captive. That was the only place he wanted to be. He jogged up the stairs three at a time and slowed when he found Claire walking out of the room. She eased the door shut. "She wants to be alone."

He tried to push past, but Claire placed her hand on his chest. "That includes you." She slid her hand around his arm and steered him to the next room over, the one he liked to commandeer when he stayed for impromptu visits.

"John, she's emotionally broken; her body is worn out from the flight; and she needs to rest." She released him and patted his chest. "Just let her sleep. I'm sure she'll want to go home soon; and I'm afraid when she sets her mind to it, there's nothing any one of us is going to be able to do to stop her."

John's heart felt as though it was squeezed in a vise grip. His gaze flew to the adjoining bathroom door.

"Just let her rest."

****

Claire left John's room and made a beeline for her husband. She found him in the library, fixing a brandy while he waited on her.

"Well?" she asked.

"He loves her."

Claire clapped her hands together. "I knew it. Oh, this is going to be the best Christmas ever."

Butch plopped down on the couch and motioned for her to join him. She slid beside him and pulled her feet under her body.

"How is she?"

"She's been through a lot. She grew up differently from John, but she's strong. She makes him a better man."

"Now, Claire, you know pushing him like this is a gamble. He could still choose the job."

She hit her husband's stomach playfully. "He wouldn't dare. He loves her. I could see it in his eyes."

"You're right. I do," John said.

Claire's mouth parted as she turned to find John standing in the hallway. He walked into the library and folded his arms across his chest.

Claire rose. "Now, John, it's not what you think."

Butch stood too. "Sure it is, kid. Your Aunt Claire is all up in your business."

Claire's mouth hung open as she glared at her husband. "I am not."

Butch tossed his arm around her shoulders and pulled her into his side. "But she means well. If you love Delaney, and you're as smart as we all know you are, then you won't let her get away. This might be the last shot you've got to win her over, kid."

John let his gaze fall to the floor. Claire didn't have to read John's mind to know what he was thinking. She'd seen uncertainty enough. He was debating whether Delaney loved him back. "She does, and I don't have to read her mind to know it."

John looked up and held his Aunt Claire's gaze. She steeled herself against poking around in his mind. This was a decision that only he could make. "I've got to run to my house. But If she comes down, tell her I'll be back."

John turned and walked out of the library.

"Butch...that maniac is still out there."

He pulled his keys out of his pocket and leaned down to give her a quick kiss. "I'm on it."

CHAPTER 14

Delaney woke in the middle of the night, when John slid into the bed with her. He pulled the covers over them both and rested his hand on her belly. "Go back to sleep, Del."

"What time is it?"

"Late, baby." He leaned in, kissed her lips, and lay back down. "I'm tired, and I just want to hold you while I sleep."

She snuggled into his arms, refusing to think about anything that would happen tomorrow. She'd cried herself to sleep thinking about her mother, what her father had taken from her, and the fact her mom wouldn't ever get to know her grandchild. The monster had stolen those precious moments.

"Close your eyes, baby," John murmured.

"John, I need to tell you something." She glanced over at him to find he was completely out. His breathing was steady; his hand on her belly was dead weight. He was definitely out. One more night, she had one more night of keeping the secret to herself.

Delaney let her eyes slide closed and, as she snuggled into the arms of the only man she'd ever let herself love, the darkness pulled her under.

****

Sleep had come peacefully for the first time in her life. She was safe behind the walls at Claire's house. Her eyes slid open and she turned to snuggle with John, her arms wrapping around his empty pillow lying beside her. The alarm clock read nine a.m. and he was already gone. She had to tell him today; he deserved to know.

She slid from the bed, took a quick shower, and dressed. She pulled her bedroom door open to find Claire, Abby, and Emma standing outside her door. Claire's hand was in the air as if she'd been about to knock.

"Oh good, you're up." Claire announced.

They all barged into the room. Delaney gestured over her shoulder with her thumb back to the door. "I was just going to go find John."

"Oh no, dear, he's with the boys, and you don't have time." Claire replied.

Abby threaded her arm through Delaney's on one side and Emma took the other. "We've planned the most wonderful day. We need to leave or we're all going to be late."

"Late for what? I don't recall making plans with any of you." Delaney asked in confusion as the other women led her downstairs and out the front door to two waiting SUVs. They all got into the first one, and she glanced back at the second. It was full with a security detail.

"Um....where are we going?"

"To get your dress for the party."

Delaney shook the fog from her head. "Claire, that's sweet, but—"

"No buts, dear. You need a dress, and then we're all going to go get our hair and makeup done while they get everything ready at the house."

Abby, who was sitting next to her in the back seat, glanced over to Delaney and whispered, "Don't argue. She'll find a way to get what she wants. It's better if you just roll with the punches."

"But I was leaving today."

"That can wait one more day, right?" Emma asked, as she turned in the passenger seat. "They haven't found your dad, and I'm sure we'll all sleep better if you wait an extra day and give Mike enough time to find him."

Delaney nibbled on her bottom lip. "I guess one more day will be fine."

"Perfect." Claire's eyes twinkled as she held Delaney's gaze in the rearview mirror. "Now let's go get beautiful. We have a long day of shopping and the spa."

Delaney let out a long breath and turned her gaze to the window.

****

"Where are they?" John called down to Butch from the top of the landing. His uncle was standing in the open entrance to the ballroom.

"They had to go get your girl a dress," Butch answered before turning around to glance up at John. "I think they mentioned shopping, the spa, makeup, nails, and hair. You know, all that girly crap."

John's eyes widened as he jogged back down the stairs. "And you thought that was a good idea with Ritchie on the loose?"

He walked over to stand next to Butch.

"I sent my best men with them, poor bastards." Butch shook his head. "They'll be fine. I have eyes inside and out. Nothing is going to happen to your girl."

He tossed his arm around John's shoulder and led him to the kitchen. "Aunt Claire had your tux put in your room and told me you wouldn't be seeing Delaney until the party."

"They're going to be gone all day?"

"Yep." Butch walked over to the coffee pot and poured them each a mug before gesturing for John to have a seat.

"Uncle Butch, can I ask you a question?"

"Sure."

Butch leaned back in the chair, steadying it on two legs.

"How did you know Aunt Claire was the one?"

The chair dropped down on all four legs. "That's easy. She's the only one who calls me on my bullshit, the only one who puts up with me."

"I'm being serious."

Butch laughed. "Me too, but besides that, I couldn't get her out of my head or my heart." He shrugged. "I needed her like I needed my next breath, and I couldn't imagine my life without her in it."

"That's how I feel about Delaney," John mumbled. "But she's so damn stubborn."

"All of the good ones are, John."

John gave a nod and rose. He walked to the sink and dumped his coffee. "I'm going to ask her to marry me." He turned to find Butch smiling. "Don't tell Aunt Claire or my mom. I want it to be a surprise tonight."

"Dixon is going to be pissed." Butch chuckled.

"Why?" John asked, unsure what his baby brother would have to do with anything.

"Because then you'll definitely be the favorite"—he grinned—"for tonight anyway."

"My brother will eventually learn that I'll always be her favorite." John chuckled. "Where are the kids going to be tonight?"

"They'll be tucked away with a couple of my best bodyguards up in our suite. I believe they're planning a rematch to beat them again in a Special Ops video game."

"You guys are going to have your hands full when they get older. You know that, right?"

"No worse than you. I seem to remember when you hated these parties just as much as they do now."

John walked out of the kitchen with an extra bounce in his step. He had plans to make and a ring to buy. His stomach twisted into knots. Doubts about her answer weighed heavily on his mind, but he pushed them to the side. There was a reason he was dreaming about Delaney Chance. She was meant to be *his* family, *his* wife.

****

Staying away from Delaney the rest of the night had been easy. His mother and aunts had held her captive the entire day, getting ready for the biggest party of the year. All of Southall would be in attendance.

They always were. John shoved one of his Glock's into the shoulder holster before securing another in the pack at his waist. He slid into his tuxedo jacket, straightening it just so. He was in his room trying to get his bow tie just right when his father walked in.

"Need help?"

"I can never get this damn thing right."

John's dad chuckled as he approached, reaching for the strands of material, he began to make the bow. "I hear you have a surprise planned for tonight."

"Damn, Uncle Butch has a big mouth."

John's dad grinned as he finished the bow, pulling at the ends. "Don't worry. I won't tell your mom." John's dad stepped back so John could look at the bow in the mirror.

"You didn't come to talk me out of it, did you?"

His dad shook his head. "Just the opposite. If you love her, never let her go. Don't make the same mistake I made with your mom. I missed all those years of watching you grow up."

John turned to his dad and noticed the sadness in his eyes. "You didn't know she was pregnant. If you had, you wouldn't have left."

He nodded. "You're right; they wouldn't have been able to tear me away." His dad placed his palm on John's shoulder. "I'm so proud of you and the man you've become. Your mom did such an amazing job..."

His dad pulled him in for a hug. Leaning out, he clasped John's arms. "Let's go get your girl."

John's dad released him and headed for the door.

"Hey, Dad."

He paused and turned around with his hand on the doorknob.

"You may not have been in my life for the first eighteen years, but I'm damn sure glad you'll be there for the rest of it."

His dad's lips tilted up into a smile. "You better do it early. It's going to be hard to keep Aunt Claire out of my head, not to mention keeping Momma Mae from appearing and telling on you."

****

John waited at the bottom of the stairs and pulled to loosen the bow around his throat, swallowing around the lump. People milled around him with champagne flutes in hand, talking. Each person announced, "Happy Holidays" as they walked past; and yet, John couldn't tear his gaze away from the stairs.

He was excusing himself from his uncle when she finally appeared. She stood at the top of the stairs in a long red ball gown. She was a vision of beauty. Her hair was twisted up the way women dressing up wore it. She met his gaze and held it. Her lips lifted into a smile, and she raised the hem of her gown as she slowly walked down the stairs toward him. It was one of those moments where everyone in the room disappeared. It was just the two of them. She was all that mattered. His heart seized in his chest when she reached the last step and smiled at him. She leaned into him, planted her lips on his, and he was home. He loved her. There was no question.

She broke the kiss and grinned. He planted his hands firmly on her waist.

"Where have you been all my life?" he asked.

"In your dreams," she replied.

"You look beautiful."

"And you don't suck yourself."

"I missed you today."

"I missed you too."

He lifted her into his arms and kissed her again, turning her so that when she slid down his body, her feet were on the ground.

John leaned back, giving her room to breathe. He took her hand and wrapped it around his arm. "Sorry about my mom and aunts. They have a way of taking over."

"So I gathered."

John led her farther into the foyer and near where all his relatives stood. They were watching John and Delaney's every movement, as if the couple was the main attraction.

"John." She pulled on his arm, turning him to look at her. "There's something I have to tell you."

"Before you say anything, let me go first."

John cleared his throat and slid the ring box out of his suit. "Delaney." He smiled despite the butterflies in his stomach and dropped down on one knee. "I know we haven't known each other long, but I hope to change that." He opened the box.

Her hand flew to her mouth, and tears welled in her eyes.

The room quieted around them, and he could hear the gasps, but he tuned everyone out.

"You stormed your way into my life and into my heart. You turned my dreams into reality, and I couldn't imagine another day of my life without you in it."

"John..."

"I love you, Delaney Chance, with all of my heart. Be my wife and let *me* be your family."

****

A tear slipped down her face. Her gaze flew around the room, panic clutched her heart. Everyone was watching. Everyone was waiting, but she couldn't say yes. Not here, not until he knew the truth.

She grabbed his hand and hauled him to his feet.

"Please excuse us," she announced while dragging him out of the room toward the terrace. She stepped outside and drew in a long, deep breath. The cool December night sent a chill through her body. She glanced back at the doors where his entire family was watching, every last one of them failing miserably to act nonchalant.

"Delaney..."

She started walking toward the outcrop of trees. "Follow me."

"Delaney, I asked you to marry me, and you want to go for a walk? Can't it wait?"

She swiveled around yet kept walking backward. "No...it can't. I've been trying to tell you something for the last week, and it's important. You need to hear what I have to say before I answer your question."

He followed as she had requested. She stopped and turned just next to the tree line beyond the garden. She held up her hand. "Not one more step, Bennett. I can't do this if you're touching me or kissing me...no. I need a clear head."

He slowed to a stop, three steps away. "Okay." He glanced back at the house. "We're alone. What is so important?"

She glanced down at her feet and drew in another deep breath.

"Del..."

She looked up. "I'm pregnant."

John's mouth parted. It wasn't the reaction she'd been expecting. She'd taken a step toward him when an arm snaked around her neck in a chokehold, the forearm pressing against her windpipe. That hand held a knife, and the metal of a barrel pressed against her temple.

"You failed at being a daughter. You'll fail at being a mother," Ritchie sneered.

John slowly reached behind him, and she knew he was going for the gun in his waistband. She'd felt it when he hugged her.

"Let her go," John demanded, the gun still behind his back.

"Don't even think about it, pig." Ritchie smirked while leaning into Delany's ear. "I'd only planned to kill you. He and your baby are just bonuses."

John's hand froze on the grip.

Ritchie turned the gun on John and pulled the trigger. The bullet pierced his left shoulder, flinging it back and twisting him. The impact dropped him to his knees.

"John!" she screamed. The whole world turned in slow motion as she watched him fall.

"You can join him," Ritchie whispered in her ear.

He removed the arm from around her throat and spun her around. The first blow came to her abdomen and the next to the chest. Her father had every intention of seeing her dead. Pain laced her body when the knife sliced through her skin. She gasped. Her lungs had a hard time pulling in a breath. Ritchie pulled the knife free and she fell to the ground. The piercing sound of gunshots filled the void as ringing started in her ears. Her body turned cold on the dewy grass. Her hand went to her stomach. Her gaze fell on her father's open, dead eyes. He had a bullet to his head. She turned her head toward John. He had a phone pressed against his ear as he inched closer to her.

"I love you," she whispered as her eyes turned heavy, the pain excruciating, to the point of dizziness. She closed her eyes to welcome the darkness.

"Del, stay with me. Help is coming," John pleaded a look of terror in his eyes as he ripped off his shirt and shred it in two, holding one portion to her stomach and the other to her chest. "Stay with me, baby." He kissed her lips, his forehead pressed against hers. "You're not allowed to die. Do you hear me! You owe me an answer."

That was the last she heard, before the darkness sucked her under.

Chapter 15

John watched in horror as the eerie vision played out in front of his eyes. The deadly dream was about to come true. The red dress and the woods, why hadn't he remembered? Ritchie stabbed Delaney. He needed a clear shot, one that didn't include Delaney or his baby getting hurt in the process. Fear raced through John's body as Ritchie stabbed her twice before tossing her to the ground like trash. It was the opening he needed, the one he'd been waiting for. He squeezed off the first round, sending a bullet through Richie's brain and then two more into his heart. One for Delaney and the other for her mother. That bastard wasn't coming back. John slid the phone out of his pocket and called his dad, talking quickly into the phone. He dropped it to the ground and inched toward her, ignoring the pain in his chest. His heart hurt more than any bullet hole.

When he reached her, his heart had almost stopped. The grass around and beneath her was soaked in blood. He ripped off his jacket and then the shirt off his back; ignoring the pain, he tore the shirt in two and pressed both pieces to her wounds. She was losing blood, too much blood. He leaned down to her.

She'd whispered I love you. She was about to give up.

"Del, stay with me. Help is coming," John pleaded while pressing the shirt tighter to her body. "Stay with me, baby." He kissed her lips, his forehead pressed against hers. "You're not allowed to die. Do you hear me! You owe me an answer."

Her lips tilted up into a small smile before her eyes slid shut.

"Help me!" John screamed toward his dad, who was running in their direction, John's mom right behind him. The rest of the family was only steps behind. His Aunt Elizabeth had kicked off her shoes and was in a full run, carrying her doctor bag with her. She ushered everyone out of the way and turned Delaney over to get a better look. She looked up at John as she furiously started pulling stuff out of her bag.

"Did she tell you?"

He nodded.

"Good. Send someone to tell the paramedics she has a stab wound through the stomach and she's pregnant."

John heard the gasps from his family, but no one spoke.

She started tearing open the gauze. "Now!" she screamed. "She's lost too much blood. Get their asses back here now."

Two of his uncles took off running around the house toward the security gate. The emergency sirens drew closer in the distance but time seemed to stand still. To John, every extra second seemed like an eternity gripping and squeezing at his heart. John helped to hold Delaney as Elizabeth tore away the back of Delaney's dress. She applied pressure with gauze to try and stop the bleeding.

Tears slid down his cheek. "Come on, baby. Come back."

He felt his mom's hands on his shoulders, her silent support something he'd known all of his life. All he needed was for Delaney to open her eyes. To tell him everything was going to be okay.

John hadn't even heard the paramedics before they were pushing him out of the way. They eased her onto the gurney and began wheeling her off, with Elizabeth leading the way.

Another paramedic had his hands on John's chest, looking at the bullet wound.

"I'm going with her," he screamed and pushed the hands away.

"They need to concentrate on her. We'll take you in the other ambulance. Just let me look at your wound."

John started walking toward the other ambulance. The adrenaline coursing through his body masked the pain. "Do it on the way."

****

John slid into one of the T-shirts his mother had brought him. His mom and dad were the only ones with him. The rest were in the OR waiting room, hoping that Elizabeth would emerge with news on Delaney's condition.

"John."

John shook his head. "I can't do this now, Mom. Delaney is in surgery and my baby..." His voice trailed off as a tear slid down his face. "I might lose them both."

"Oh, John" His mother eased her arms around him, careful not to hurt him.

"She'll be okay. They both will." She leaned out of his hold. Tears streaked down her face. "She's meant to be a Bennett. They both are. She's going to make it."

"Mom, what if she doesn't?" His shoulders shook as the tears flowed. "What if she doesn't?"

Abby swiped the tears from her face. "Whatever happens, we'll handle this together, like we've always done. You have to stay positive."

He nodded.

The nurse walked in and handed him the instructions on how to care for his wound, and then John slid off the emergency room bed. His dad had his mother held tightly against his side.

"Now, we wait." John walked out of the room and headed toward the elevators. He stabbed the button and waited for the ding. The elevator arrived only seconds later, but they seemed like the longest minutes of his life. He needed to get to the OR waiting room. What if she woke up and he wasn't there? What if she had to deal with losing the baby and he wasn't there for her? He'd never forgive himself. Not ever.

His mother laced her arm through his. His father walked in silence behind them as they entered the room. His aunts came out of their chairs, each taking a turn to pull him into her arms.

"Is there any word?"

"No," Butch answered. "We're still waiting."

John turned toward Aunt Emma. "Are there any new ghosts floating around?"

Emma gave a reassuring shake of her head.

"Good."

Everyone sat back down in the chairs, but not John. He paced the floor as if he were an expectant father. Hell, he was. He rubbed his hand over his head and sat down next to his dad. Minutes turned into an hour, and that turned into several. He sent his aunts and uncles home. They were still dressed in their tuxedos and gowns. He assured them he'd call when he got word. They'd promised to go home, change, and come right back, and then reluctantly left.

His family was like no other. His mother and father walked down to the cafeteria to get coffee for all of them, and John was left alone with his thoughts. He stood and had started pacing when he spotted Elizabeth standing in the doorway. She removed the cloth covering her mouth and let out a long breath.

"Well?" John asked, hurrying to her.

"A punctured lung and a two broken ribs. She lost a lot of blood, and we had to give her a transfusion."

"Is she going to be okay?" John's heart clenched tight in his chest.

Elizabeth rubbed his arm. "She'll be fine. We're going to keep her in ICU, but it's more for observation than anything else."

John's legs turned to noodles, and he would have fallen had Elizabeth not guided him over to sit in a chair.

"And the baby?"

She glanced over her shoulder. "Where's your mom? I think she needs to be here for this."

"Aunt Elizabeth. Just tell me. How is my baby?"

Elizabeth took a deep breath and took John's hands in hers. "Your baby is fine. Actually better than fine. Given what I know about you Bennett's, I would say he or she appears to be surrounded by some type of protective barrier.

"You mean the amnio sac?"

Elizabeth shook her head. "No. With the trajectory of the lower knife wound and the damage in Delaney's body, by all accounts, the knife should have killed your child."

John shook his head. "I don't understand."

She glanced back toward the doorway as if to check that they were still alone. "I think the baby is gifted. There is no other explanation. I simply don't know, and you know how much I hate saying that. But it's the truth. I don't know how the baby survived. He has to have some type of protection ability."

A tear slid down John's face. "Protection?"

Elizabeth nodded. "And I honestly think whatever ability your child has, or that protective bubble actually stopped the knife from going farther; he protected himself. I also think he did the same with her chest wound. There was minimal damage there also.

"The baby saved her life?" John placed his head in his hands, trying to let the information sink in.

He looked up. "When can I see her?"

Elizabeth glanced at her watch. "We're keeping her in ICU so it's supposed to be during visiting hours, but I pulled a few strings for you. Under the circumstances, I think it best if you're there when she comes to. I had a cot put in the room. I just have to warn you, nurses will be coming in during the night. You won't get much sleep."

John rose. "I don't care." He hugged Elizabeth and whispered into her ear, "Thank you."

"Aw, honey. I just patched the wounds. I think the baby did all of the work."

John followed Elizabeth into the ICU where the rooms were open and all of them faced the nurses' station. Elizabeth hadn't been kidding when she said he wouldn't get any sleep. Not that he would have anyway - until he saw her eyes.

"Have a seat. I'm going to go find your mom and dad. I'm sure everyone else would be happy to hear the news."

John nodded and pulled a chair up next to Delaney's bed. He held her hand and listened to the beep of the machines, beeps that meant both Delaney and the baby were alive.

John closed his eyes and said a silent prayer. John stayed by her side, holding her hand as long as his eyes would allow. He needed the connection, the closeness. He needed her.

At about three a.m., one of the nurses woke him and had him move to the cot. He closed his eyes and immediately began to dream.

Delaney stood in a field of green grass, holding a little girl's hand. They turned around as if they were surprised he was there.

"Daddy," the little girl yelled and ran into John's arms, practically knocking him over.

John's eyes flew open.

Nurses milled in and out of the room, checking machines and Delaney's vital signs. One nurse repositioned the monitor around Del's belly, a monitor that was tracking the baby's stats. John wiped the sleep from his eyes and sat up. He glanced at his watch and saw it was four o'clock in the morning. He stood, arched his back in a stretch, and moved back into the chair next to the bed. He placed a kiss on her hand and rested his chin on the bed.

Aunt Elizabeth walked into the room and picked up Delaney's chart.

"Why hasn't she woken up?" John asked.

Elizabeth moved farther into the room, picking up the ribbons of paper the machine was printing out. "She suffered a severe trauma. She needs her rest."

Elizabeth moved about the room, checking all of the machines as she went.

"Shouldn't you be at home and in bed?" John asked. "I'm sure Uncle Mike is missing you."

She shook her head and smiled. "I'm exactly where I need to be." She wrote a few things on Delaney's chart before placing a reassuring hand on his shoulder. "She should be awake soon, but I'll keep checking back."

"Thank you."

She left John alone in the room, alone with his thoughts, alone with his worry. He cupped his hands over Delaney's and laid his head down on top. He didn't know how long he had stayed that way, but he felt her fingers twitch.

His head shot up, and the most beautiful sight he'd ever seen stared back at him. Her eyes were bloodshot, and her look worried. She moved her other hand over her stomach. "The baby?"

John stood and leaned over to press his lips first to hers and then placed a kiss on her belly. "The baby is fine. She saved your life."

Delaney's brows dipped. She rubbed her chapped lips, and John grabbed the pitcher of water by the bed and poured her a glass. He held it up to her lips and let her sip.

He could read the relief in her eyes. She cleared her throat. "How is that possible?"

John shook his head. "I'll tell you about it when you're more awake. Just know that the baby is fine; you're going to be fine; and now, I can breathe again."

She placed her palm on his cheek and held his gaze with a look of pure and utter love. "Yes. The answer is yes."

John's shoulders relaxed. The need to crawl up and lie with her in the bed was overwhelming, but he knew better than to even try. "Let's get you all better so I can take you home."

She smiled and nodded before closing her eyes again.

Chapter 16

Delaney shot off a text from her phone before she eased down onto the couch next to her husband. The last eight months had been a flurry of excitement. She'd gotten married. They'd built a new house and set up a room for the baby. Her new extended family had been so helpful and loving, accepting her like one of their own. And John, she was so thankful for John. He was an amazing man and such a caring husband. There was no man in the world that could hold a candle to the one she'd married. So much had changed in her life. With the death of her father came inheritance from offshore accounts. The asshole would be rolling over in his grave had he known that Delaney was the last living heir to the fortune of blood money he'd left behind. She'd done what any good daughter, who despised her father, would have done. She donated the ten million dollars to a charity that specialized in helping women like her mother escape abusive spouses. Delaney grinned at the memory.

John wrapped his arm around Delaney, pulling her closer to snuggle into his side.

"You okay?" he asked.

That was a question she could go without ever hearing again.

"Yeah, you?"

He kissed her forehead and pointed the remote control at the TV. "It's your choice tonight. What sappy love story are we watching?"

Delaney rubbed her hand over her belly. The contractions were coming closer together and it was almost time for them to go.

"How about the one where you meet your daughter?"

The flipping of channels paused. "What? Is it time?"

"Yes." She grinned and leaned up to kiss his lips.

John's eyes widened and his body tensed.

"Don't panic, Bennett. I've already sent a text to Elizabeth. She's going to be waiting for us at the hospital."

John shook the confusion from his mind and eased out from beneath her. "We have to go."

She could hear the excitement in his voice.

"We have to go now. Are you okay to walk or should I carry you?" John asked while spinning in place, his gaze darting around the room.

"I can walk if you can help me up." He helped ease her up and kept a grip on her elbow as if afraid she might fall.

"You aren't going to drive like a bat out of hell, are you? Should I call your mom?"

"No...yes."

She tried to stifle her grin. "Which is it?"

"No, I'll take you to the hospital and, yes, you can call my mother on the way. She'd kill us if we didn't."

Delaney and John were out the door and in the car before she could reply. "I'm sure the others already know."

His cell phone chose that minute to ring, and he hit the Bluetooth in the car as he drove ever so cautiously and ever so fast en route to the hospital.

"Bennett," he answered.

"Delaney's mother and Momma Mae keep popping in and out. Everything okay?"

"It's time," Delaney announced while trying to breathe through the next set of contractions.

"Oh my God, okay. I'll tell the others." Emma disconnected the call.

John's grip on the wheel had turned his fingers white. She reached over and placed her palm on his arm. "Everything is going to be okay," she said reassuringly.

"I know," John announced. "She came to me last night."

"Aw...I love that she visits you in your dreams but, if you don't hurry, she's going to be visiting you in the SUV." Delaney moaned louder when the next contraction hit.

****

John cradled his daughter in his arms. The rocking motion of the chair had eased her into a deep sleep. Her tiny hand was wrapped around one of his fingers in a vise grip. Delaney was propped up in the hospital bed. She was smiling as she watched them both. He held her gaze. "I love you, Delaney. Chloe and you are my world."

"And to think none of this would have happened had you not purchased my dagger. What super power do you think she has?"

He glanced back down at his sleeping daughter. "I'm not sure. I don't think we'll know until she shows some signs of something."

"I can tell you at least one," Claire announced while leaning on the frame in the doorway. She pushed off and entered the room. "I didn't mean to eavesdrop."

John met Delaney's gaze. "Yes, she did."

Delaney nodded. "I thought you could only read minds, not predict the future."

Claire waved her hand in the air while moving to stand behind John for a better look at the baby. "Telepathy." Claire reached down and tucked the blanket tighter around the baby. "She's cold."

Delaney closed her eyes and leaned back into the pillows. "She's talking to you?"

"She's talking to all of us," Abby announced as she walked into the room. "Sorry, Del, but I'm afraid you're going to have your hands full with this one."

"Well, I already knew that. She's a Bennett, for goodness sake."

Abby winked. "So are you."

ABOUT THE AUTHOR

Kate has lived in Florida for most of her entire life. She enjoys a quiet life with her husband and two kids.

Kate has pulled all-nighters finishing her favorite books and also writing them. She says she'll sleep when she's dead or when her muse stops singing off key.

She loves creating worlds full of suspense, secrets, hunky men, kick ass heroines, steamy sex and oh yeah the love of a lifetime. Not to mention an occasional ghost and other supernatural talents thrown into the mix.

Kate Allenton